*She'd gotten emotionally involved
with Craig and his sons.*

Jill knew better, but she'd done it anyway.

She'd wanted it to be real. All of it. Craig's
affection. And the boys' feelings, too. She liked
taking care of them. She liked being the one they
confessed their secrets to, the one they ran to when
they were hurting.

After years of being lonely, her heart had
responded to the love between the boys and their
father. She'd wanted a piece of that for herself.
Was that so wrong?

Jill knew the answer. Of course it was.

Because it wasn't real.

She was, after all, just the hired help.

Wasn't she?

Dear Reader,

Weddings, wives, fathers—and, of course, Moms—are in store this May from Silhouette Special Edition!

As popular author Susan Mallery demonstrates, Jill Bradford may be a *Part-Time Wife*, but she's also May's THAT SPECIAL WOMAN! She has quite a job ahead of her trying to tame a HOMETOWN HEARTBREAKER.

Also this month Leanne Banks tells a wonderful tale of an *Expectant Father*. In fact, this hero's instant fatherhood is anything but expected—as is finding his true love! Two new miniseries get under way this month. First up is the new series by Andrea Edwards, GREAT EXPECTATIONS. Three sisters and three promises of love—and it begins this month with *On Mother's Day*. Sweet Hope is the name of the town, and bells are ringing for some SWEET HOPE WEDDINGS in this new series by Amy Frazier. Don't miss book one, *New Bride in Town*. Rounding out the month is *Rainsinger* by Ruth Wind and Allison Hayes's debut book for Special Edition, *Marry Me, Now!*

I know you won't want to miss a minute of the month of May from Silhouette Special Edition. It's sure to put a spring in your step this springtime!

Sincerely,

Tara Gavin
Senior Editor

Please address questions and book requests to:
Silhouette Reader Service
U.S.: 3010 Walden Ave., P.O. Box 1325, Buffalo, NY 14269
Canadian: P.O. Box 609, Fort Erie, Ont. L2A 5X3

# SUSAN MALLERY

## PART-TIME WIFE

*Silhouette*®

**SPECIAL EDITION**®

Published by Silhouette Books
America's Publisher of Contemporary Romance

To Tara Gavin—for giving me the opportunity to write books that make me laugh, make me cry, and best of all, books that make me believe anything is possible.
My appreciation and my thanks.

 SILHOUETTE BOOKS

ISBN 0-373-24027-9

PART-TIME WIFE

Copyright © 1996 by Susan W. Macias

This edition published by arrangement with Harlequin Books S.A.

® and TM are trademarks of Harlequin Books S.A., used under license. Trademarks indicated with ® are registered in the United States Patent and Trademark Office, the Canadian Trade Marks Office and in other countries.

Printed in U.S.A.

**Books by Susan Mallery**

Silhouette Special Edition

*Tender Loving Care* #717
*More Than Friends* #802
*A Dad for Billie* #834
*Cowboy Daddy* #898
*The Best Bride* #933
*Marriage on Demand* #939
*Father In Training* #969
*The Bodyguard & Ms. Jones* #1008
*Part-Time Wife* #1027

*Hometown Heartbreakers

Silhouette Intimate Moments

*Tempting Faith* #554
*The Only Way Out* #646

## SUSAN MALLERY

makes her home in the Lone Star State where the people are charming and the weather is always interesting. She lives with her hero-material husband and her attractive but not very bright cats. When she's not hard at work writing romances, she can be found exploring the wilds of Texas and shopping for the perfect pair of cowboy boots. Susan writes historical romances under the name Susan Macias. You may write to her directly at P.O. Box 1828, Sugar Land, TX 77487.

## Jill's Famous Prune Bread

1 cup dried prunes, chopped
1 cup orange juice
1 cup whole wheat flour
1 cup all purpose flour
½ cup sugar
3 tsp baking powder
¼ tsp salt
½ tsp ground cinnamon
2 beaten eggs
1 Tbsp vegetable oil
½ cup chopped nuts

Combine prunes and juice; let stand ½ hour. Stir together dry ingredients in a separate bowl. Combine eggs, oil and prune mixture; add to dry ingredients, mixing well. Add nuts. Turn into a greased 9x5x3-inch loaf pan. Bake at 350° F for 35 minutes. Remove from pan and cool. Serves 8-10 adults, or 4 teenage boys.

## Chapter One

At the exact moment the hot water kicked on in the shower, the doorbell rang. Jill Bradford leaned her forehead against the ceramic tile and gritted her teeth. Timing. Life was all about timing and hers was usually bad.

Or maybe it was this house, she thought, grabbing her robe with one hand while she turned off the water with the other. Maybe there was a little light that ran from the bathroom to the front of the building so that every time she tried to take a shower, it went on. People saw the light and knew it was time to come calling. Yesterday it had been young girls selling cookies. Two days ago, someone selling magazine subscriptions.

The bell rang again, and Jill hurried down the hall. She had the fleeting thought that she could not bother with her robe and could simply flash whoever was rude enough to interrupt her shower, but decided against the idea. The way her luck was running, there would be a cop on the other side of the door and she would be arrested.

She reached the front door just as the visitor pressed the bell again. This time the long tone sounded impatient. Jill raised herself up on her toes and stared out the tiny peephole that had obviously been designed by and for the tall people of the world. She stared at the distorted image and gasped.

A cop?

Barely pausing long enough to secure the tie on her robe, she turned the key to release the dead bolt and jerked open the door. "Yes?"

"Ms. Jill Bradford?"

"Yes."

"I'm Craig Haynes."

The police officer paused as if the name was supposed to mean something. Jill stared at him and blinked. It didn't mean a thing to her. She studied the man. He was tall. Too tall for her comfort. She had to crane her head back to see his face. But it was worth the crick in her neck, she decided, taking in curly dark hair, brown eyes and features handsome enough to grace a male model. She inspected the shape of his mouth and the stubborn set of his chin. She didn't have a perfect memory but she was reasonably confident she would have remembered someone who looked as good as he did.

Her gaze slipped down his chest. The black short-sleeved shirt of his uniform outlined his well-muscled body. He had the build of an athlete. Impressive. Very impressive. Even to someone who had sworn off men and relationships.

"I'm sorry, Officer Haynes," she said, returning her attention to his face. "I don't know who you are."

The faint hints of gray at his temples were the only clue he wasn't as young as he appeared. He didn't look thirty, but she would guess he was several years older than that.

He chose that moment to smile. Lines appeared around his eyes and mouth. His teeth flashed white. He should come with a warning label, she thought as her stomach clenched and her knees threatened to buckle. *Do not operate heavy machinery around this man.* If she hadn't been leaning against the doorframe, she would have collapsed in a heap at his feet.

"I should have been more specific," he said. "Your friend Kim gave me your name. She was going to take care of my kids. She said you would be happy to take her place."

Kids? "Oh, now I remember." Jill smiled. "Of course." She pushed the door open wide. "Sorry. Please come in, and we can talk about this."

"Thanks." He stepped past her into the small entryway. The view from the back was pretty impressive, too, she thought as she gave him a quick once-over. Wide shoulders and the kind of butt most women would kill to have. Why was it men had great butts simply by virtue of being men, while women could aerobicize until their hearts were strong enough to power a freight train but the shape was never quite right? Not that Jill spent all that much time on the treadmill. Still, she thought about it a lot and surely that counted for something.

"In here," she said, motioning for Craig to step into the living room.

He moved with an easy long-legged stride. She felt like a dwarf waddling along behind him. Not that she was heavy. She was just short. And curvy. An unfortunate combination that made her feel like a cuddly kitten in a world full of Barbie dolls.

The perfect creases in his uniform pants, and the carefully trimmed dark hair that stopped just above his collar, made her remember her own disheveled appearance. She touched her short hair and tried to remember how much it had been sticking up the last time she'd looked in a mirror.

"You'll have to excuse me," she said, perching on the edge of the sofa. Craig had chosen the wing chair opposite the fireplace. He leaned forward and placed his uniform cap brim-up on the coffee table. "I've been so busy taking care of things for Kim I haven't had a chance to shower this morning."

She tugged on the hem of her suddenly too-short robe and tried to look mature. She was thirty, but without makeup and tailored clothes, she looked like a teenager. Her mother had told her that in time she would appreciate looking so young, but Jill wasn't sure. She had a bad feeling she was still going to look like a cute, albeit wrinkled, kitten well into her seventies. The tall world did not take short people seriously.

"When did Kim leave?" Craig asked.

"They eloped yesterday." She smiled, remembering her friend's happiness. Kim hadn't been sure it was the right thing to do, but Jill had encouraged her to go. Real love, the forever kind, didn't come around very often. Jill might have had her heart broken more times than any one woman deserved, but she still had faith— for other people, if not for herself.

"It was very romantic," she continued. "Brian hired a limo to take them to the airport. She'd told a few friends, so they were here to see them off."

She stared out the window, but instead of the front yard and the house across the street, she saw the radiant couple. The love between them had been as tangible as the small bouquet Kim had been holding.

"She called last night from Reno, and they're already married. She should be back in a couple of weeks."

There was a manila folder on top of the glass coffee table. Jill reached for it and flipped it open. There were several sheets of papers covered with careful notes. Lists of people to call, bills to pay, errands to run. She didn't mind. It was the least she could do for a friend. After all, when her life had fallen apart, Kim had offered her a place to stay. Speaking of which, Brian would be moving into Kim's house after the honeymoon. Jill needed to start looking for a place of her own.

Later, she told herself, scanning the list. Craig Haynes. Oh, there he was. Right between canceling a dentist's appointment and checking on the delivery of Kim's new king-size bed.

"Here's the note," she said, then glanced up at Craig.

The police officer had the oddest look on his face. As if he'd never seen anyone like her before. She reached up and fingered the ends of her short hair. Was it sticking up in spikes? Did she still have crumbs from her Pop-Tart toaster pastry around her mouth?

She licked her lips but didn't feel anything. Craig's gaze narrowed and his back stiffened. She almost asked what was wrong, but figured she probably didn't really want to know. She glanced back at the list.

"Jill said you have three boys. Twelve, nine and six. That's really not a problem for me."

She made the statement brightly. Someone who didn't know her wouldn't notice the tightness around the words. No one would be able to feel her heart beating faster. Baby-sitting. There were a thousand other things she would have gladly done for Kim instead, like regrout the shower or put down a tile floor. But she hadn't been given a choice. Still, it was just for a couple of nights. She would survive.

A wave of longing swept over her. She missed her girls. Her fingers tightened on the papers she was holding. They weren't her girls, she reminded herself. She'd just been their stepmother. She must not have been a very good one, either, because ever since the divorce, neither of the girls had wanted to see her. But the pain wasn't enough to stop her from missing them.

"Not so fast," Craig said, leaning forward in the wing chair.

"Hmm? What?" She blinked away the past and focused on the very good-looking man sitting in front of her. "What do you mean?"

"Have you done this sort of thing before?" he asked.

"Taken care of children? Of course. I was a teenager, Officer Haynes. I baby-sat." She thought of mentioning her failed marriage but figured it wasn't his business.

"You're not employed now." It was a statement.

She felt a faint flush on her cheeks. "No. I left my last position a couple of months ago."

"Were you fired?"

"No! Of course not. I just needed to get away. It's more like a leave of absence. I have an open invitation to return if I want to."

His dark gaze held hers. "The name of the company you worked for?"

"McMillian Insurance in San Clemente. That's Southern California."

"I know where it is." He pulled a small notebook and pen from his shirt pocket and wrote. "Who did you report to there?"

She gave him the name and phone number, then frowned. "Excuse me, Officer Haynes, but I don't understand why you're interrogating me."

"It's Craig, and I'm not going to trust just anyone with my children."

"I appreciate that. I assure you I'm not a convicted felon and—"

"Are you an accused felon?" The corner of his mouth tilted up with a hint of a smile.

"Not that either. I haven't even had a parking ticket in years. My point is, I'm going to be looking after your children for one or two nights. While I appreciate your diligence, I think you're taking it a little too far. I'm hardly going to be an influential force in their lives."

"Is that what you think? Ms. Bradford—"

"Jill," she interrupted.

He nodded. "Jill, I'm not looking for a baby-sitter. Kim had agreed to be a live-in nanny for my three boys. When she decided to elope, she said you'd take the job."

"Well, she was wrong," Jill said without thinking.

A full-time nanny? That was insane. Absolutely the last thing she wanted was to work with someone else's kids. Okay, she didn't have a job right now, but that was because she wasn't sure what she wanted to do with her life. She could go back to San Clemente. Her condo was sublet, but she could rent another one. Her job was waiting. But that didn't feel right. She didn't want to go back to her old life. That was the point of living with Kim for a few weeks.

Craig moved to the edge of the chair. He rested his elbows on his knees and clasped his hands together, clutching the notebook. "Jill, I'm in a bind. I've interviewed literally a dozen women for the position, and Kim was the only one I thought would work. She was young enough to be able to relate to the children and old enough to maintain discipline. She assured me you had experience with children and would be just as suitable. She also said you'd agreed to take her place."

"I said I would baby-sit. She never told me it was a full-time job. My Lord, you probably want me to live with you and your boys."

He nodded. His dark eyebrows drew together. "I'm currently involved in a special investigation. I won't bore you with the details, but it requires me to be gone odd hours. I never know when I'm going to be called away. The boys are too young to be left alone. They need some stability. I've had five nannies in the last four months."

She frowned. "What's wrong with your children?"

He hesitated just long enough for her to suspect there really *was* a problem. "My wife and I divorced several years ago. Although she didn't have much contact with them, her death last year shook them up. The woman who had looked after them left shortly after that. Since then it's been one change after another. With my new assignment and being gone all the time—" He turned his hands palms up and spread his fingers. "They're scared little kids who need someone to look after them. Nothing more."

She rose to her feet and walked to the window. "You're not playing fair," she said slowly, staring at the house across the street. "I have this mental picture of poor starving orphans shivering in the snow."

"Based on the weekly food bill, they're not starving."

Jill grimaced. Damn him, and damn Kim. When her friend returned from her honeymoon, Jill was going to give her a piece of her mind. This wasn't fair. Not to Jill, not to Craig and not to the kids.

She fought against a twinge of guilt. She was partially to blame. When Kim had come to her and talked about eloping, Jill had encouraged her to just go for it. Her life was so upside-down, she wanted someone she cared about to be happy. Kim had worried about the job, and Jill had blithely told her she would step in.

Next time I'll find out the details before agreeing, Jill promised herself. In the meantime, three boys didn't have anyone to look after them.

"I find it difficult to believe that you couldn't find one other nanny you liked," Jill said.

Craig didn't answer. She turned to face him and found him standing only a few feet behind her. She had to tilt her head back to meet his gaze.

"I've taken enough of your time," he said and placed his hat on his head. The black uniform emphasized his dark hair and eyes.

He was leaving. That would be best for both of them. Yet what about the children? She really didn't have a job right now, and she wasn't ready to go back to San Clemente. She might never be ready to do that.

Besides, she could use the money. If it wasn't permanent, if she were careful to keep her heart firmly under lock and key, it might not be so bad. She would be a caretaker; she would not get personally involved.

"Spring break is in a few weeks," she said quickly. "Let's give each other a one-week trial. If it works out, I'll stay until break. That will give you time to find someone who wants a permanent position. Agreed?"

He stared down at her. She couldn't read his expression. She wondered how much of that was because he was a cop and how much of it was the man himself. He didn't look like the chatty, outgoing type.

He crossed to her in two long strides and held out his hand. "Agreed."

His smile once again made her knees threaten to buckle. At least she was short enough that if she collapsed it wasn't a real long way down. She extended her hand toward him and tried to give him *her* best smile. He didn't seem the least bit affected. Hmm, she would have to work on it more. She wanted to leave men in a broken heap trailing behind her. Maybe it was—

His skin brushed against hers. Instantly electricity raced between them. His long fingers and broad palm swallowed her hand nearly up to her wrist. Her heart thundered in double time and her breathing choked to a stop. She hoped she didn't look as stunned as she felt. She hoped it was just a quirk of fate, a not-to-be-repeated cosmic thing, because there was no way she was going to get involved with a man. Any man. And certainly not one with children.

Been there, done that, she reminded herself. The punishing aftermath was still evident in her healing emotional wounds.

"Do you have a car?" Craig asked, apparently un-fazed by the sparks leaping between them. Or maybe they were just leaping one way.

"Uh-huh." She withdrew her hand and, before she could stop herself, wiped it on her robe. The soft cotton did nothing to erase the electricity still prickling her skin.

He raised his eyebrows but didn't say anything. She was grateful.

"If you want to pack a few things, we could go right over." He glanced at his watch. "My neighbor could only stay with the boys for an hour."

"They're home today?"

"It's Saturday."

"Oh. I forgot." With the excitement of getting Kim ready to elope, there hadn't been time to keep track of mundane things like days of the week. "No problem." She glanced down at her robe. "Let me take a quick shower and pack enough to last until Monday. I can come back here while they're in school. I still have a few things to take care of for Kim."

She started toward the doorway, then glanced at him. "You can have a seat. Or there's coffee in the kitchen. Whatever."

"I'll wait here," he said.

She stepped into the hallway.

"Jill?"

She turned around. He'd removed his hat and was running his hand through his hair. His self-control slipped a bit, and she saw the worry in his eyes. "I hope Kim knows what a good friend you are. You didn't have to do this. I really appreciate it."

The compliment made her uncomfortable. "No big deal. I'm a sucker for kids and puppies. Be right out."

Even as she hurried up the stairs, she started making a mental list of everything she would have to do. Packing, stopping the paper. She wouldn't worry about the mail today. But Monday she would put it on vacation hold. Kim didn't have any pets, which made that part easy. She would tell Kim's neighbor she was leaving so someone would keep an eye on the house. She would need Craig's phone number, too.

She walked into the guest bathroom and closed the door behind her. As she glanced into the mirror, she stifled a groan. Her hair *was* sticking up in spiky tufts. Her mother had promised her it would darken as she got older, but it was still the color of a rag doll's. She wore it short because otherwise she looked out of proportion. Without makeup, her eyes looked too big and green. That, combined with her small, almost triangular button nose, gave her an uncomfortable resemblance to the kitten so many people likened her to.

"I'll just pencil in some whiskers and be done with it," she muttered under her breath, then turned her back on the image and flipped on the shower. No wonder Craig Haynes had hired her. She looked young enough to be the perfect playmate for his kids.

Craig drew in a deep breath and let it out slowly. Now that Jill had left the room, he was able to ease up on his iron-willed self-control. It was as if the dam burst, as heated blood coursed through his body, settling inappropriately in his groin. He walked to the window and stared out blindly. He hoped his new nanny believed in taking long showers. He was going to need the extra time to get himself back under control.

He could handle the fact that she was an attractive woman, although the petite pixie look had never been his type. Big green eyes and a smile that promised two parts humor and one part sin was okay with him, too. The tousled just-out-of-bed look was a bit more of a problem, but he knew he would have been able to keep it all together... if she hadn't been naked.

He swore under his breath. He'd been so worried about the boys, he hadn't noticed at first. But when she'd settled on the sofa, her full breasts had been evident beneath the thin fabric of her robe. He hadn't had a date in two years. He hadn't been with a woman for even longer. Unfortunately, his body had chosen that moment to surge back to life.

Even with her out of the room and only the faint hint of her perfume lingering in the air, he could feel the need flowing through him. He wanted to go to her and hold her in his arms. He wanted to kiss her and—

"Stop it," he said aloud.

He had to get control. All that mattered was finding someone to take care of the boys. Jill Bradford was only a stopgap. He was going to have to find someone permanent. As if he had the time.

He rubbed the back of his neck. The dull ache that began between his shoulder blades and worked its way up his neck had become a permanent companion. Now it stepped up a degree in intensity. He would start interviewing right away. The agency swore they didn't have anyone else to send him, but there had to be someone. Maybe the perfect nanny was about to leave her job somewhere else. He could only hope.

He heard footsteps overhead. He thought about all he knew about Jill. Kim had mentioned she was recovering from a messy divorce. He could relate to that.

He'd gone through the same thing nearly six years ago. Krystal had wanted out, but she hadn't made it easy. He'd hung on as best he could, trying to be both mother and father to the boys. He'd thought he was doing well, until this last year.

What had gone wrong? Was it the hours he put in? He didn't usually volunteer for special assignments, but this one was different. There wasn't a lot of glory involved. No big drug busts, no fifteen minutes of fame on the local news report. Just directly helping those in need. He'd wanted to give something back. Were his kids paying the price for that?

He knew some of the trouble with the boys was that they'd lost Mrs. Miller. She'd been a part of their lives for nearly five years. Coming on the heels of their mother's death— Craig shook his head. No wonder the boys weren't themselves.

He'd done his best to keep it from happening, but history was repeating itself again. He was gone a lot, as *his* father had been. He was failing his kids, and he wasn't sure how to make it better.

A thunk from the top of the stairs broke through his musings. He walked through the living room and into the hallway. Jill was dragging down a suitcase almost as big as she was.

"I'll get that," he said, taking the stairs two at a time.

"I can manage," she said politely, then stood aside to let him pick up the case. It wasn't very heavy, but she was so tiny, how big could her clothes be?

"Is this it?" he asked when he reached the first floor.

She nodded. "I can come back and get whatever I've forgotten." She had a purse over her shoulder. She shook it once, then frowned. "Keys. I need keys."

While she glanced at the small table in the entryway, then patted her pockets, he studied her. She'd made a quick change. Her short red hair was still damp from her shower. Bangs fell nearly to her delicate eyebrows. The style left her small ears bare. She'd put on some makeup. With it, she looked older, although not anywhere near thirty, which he knew she was. She wore faded jeans that hinted at the curvy legs he'd seen just a few minutes before. The baggy white sweatshirt dwarfed her small frame. She'd pushed up the sleeves, exposing finely boned hands and wrists.

He had the uncomfortable feeling that a man as big as himself could easily crush her if he wasn't careful.

"My keys," she muttered, shaking her purse again. "Come on, Jill, you usually have it together."

"But do you usually talk to yourself?" he asked.

She looked startled, as if she'd forgotten he was there. Then she grinned. "Yeah, I usually do. Sorry. You and the boys will have to get used to it."

"Don't worry. I talk to myself, too. A hazard of the job. Too much time alone." He motioned toward the front door. "Are those your keys in the lock?"

She turned around and stared. "Oh. Thanks."

He pulled them free. "Not a good idea to keep them here. If someone breaks in you want to make it hard, not easy. By leaving the keys in the door, you let him walk out the front, like he belongs here." He shifted the keys until he held the one to her car. "Not to mention giving him a nice late-model vehicle to steal."

"Yeah, yeah, I know. But if I don't keep them in the door, I lose them."

"You lost them anyway."

She stared at him, then reached for her keys. He let them fall in her palm, rather than risk direct contact. Her expression turned thoughtful.

"Craig, do you ever go off duty?"

"Not usually."

"How do the boys feel about that?"

Her green eyes saw too much, he thought grimly. He raised the suitcase slightly. "Do you need anything else?" he asked.

"Nope. I'm ready." She followed him out onto the porch, then locked the door behind them. "What, no patrol car?"

He pointed to his two-year-old Honda. "Sorry, no. There's a utility vehicle at the house so you can cart the boys and their sports equipment around, but I use this to get back and forth to the station."

Her red Mustang convertible was parked in the driveway. She opened the trunk and he set the suitcase inside. "Get many tickets in this?" he asked.

"It looks flashy, but I never drive fast. I know that's disappointing, but at heart I'm pretty boring."

He was about to tell her he wouldn't have used that word to describe her. Cute, maybe. Tempting, probably. Sexy, definitely. But boring? Not in this lifetime. And any man who thought that obviously had his head up his—

He cleared his throat. "I live south of here. In Fern Hill."

"I'm not familiar with the neighborhood."

"It's an independent city. You'll like it. Just follow me. I'll go slow."

Her gaze widened, as if she'd read more into his statement than he'd meant. Before he could explain, she smiled. "Okay, Officer Haynes, I'll be right behind you." She opened the driver's door and slid inside.

As Craig started his car and pulled away from the curb, he thought about what Kim had said when she'd phoned to tell him she couldn't take the job.

"I have a friend who would be perfect for you."

In that moment, on a night when the pressures of the job and raising three kids alone had driven him to the edge of his patience, he'd wanted to believe she referred to more than a baby-sitter.

"Pretty stupid, Haynes," he muttered. He'd given up on relationships a long time ago. There weren't any promises, no sure things. And his ex-wife, Krystal, had taught him the foolishness of trying to believe in love.

So what if he found Jill attractive? All that meant was he wasn't as dead inside as he'd thought. Maybe it was time to think about dating. There was only one problem. He came from a long line of men particularly gifted at screwing up relationships.

## Chapter Two

Craig pulled up in front of the house and motioned for Jill to park her car in the driveway. He pushed the button on the garage door opener and got out immediately, but she sat in her red Mustang, staring. He glanced at the two-story home in front of him. It wasn't all that different from his neighbors'. The area was a more recent development, about six years old. He'd bought the house after his divorce, thinking that making a clean break would make it easier for all the boys. Besides, Fern Hill had a great school system with a sports program that was the envy of the state. He'd wanted that for his sons.

He tried to see the house as a stranger would see it. The high peaked roof was Spanish tile, as were most of the others on the street. White stucco with wood accents, tall windows that—he squinted and stared—needed washing pretty badly. The front yard was oversized, mowed but not trimmed. He frowned. Since taking his temporary assignment, he hadn't spent much time at home. The house showed the neglect. He wondered if the boys did, too.

Jill stepped out of her car and gave him a slight smile. "Cops make more money than I thought," she said. "This is nice."

"It's south of the city," he said, "so most people won't make the commute. For me, it's closer to work and closer to Glenwood, where my brothers live."

"Great." But she didn't sound very enthused.

She walked around to the rear of her car and lifted the trunk. Before she could reach for the suitcase, he grabbed it and pulled it out.

This time her smile was genuine. "Thanks. Such nice manners. Your mother must be proud."

Before he had to decide whether to explain that he hadn't seen his mother in years, the front door was flung open and two boys raced down the walkway. Craig grinned when he saw them.

"Is this her?" C.J. asked. His nine-year-old looked like a typical Haynes male, with dark hair and eyes.

"Yes. Jill, this is my middle son, C.J. Short for—"

She looked at the boy and winked. "Let me guess," she said, interrupting. "Craig Junior."

"Yeah." C.J. skittered to a stop in front of her and held out his hand. "Pleased to meet you, Ms. Bradford. I'm very much looking forward to having you as our nanny."

She looked at Craig. "Impressive."

He shrugged. "C.J.'s our charmer."

"And a fine job he does, too." She took the hand the boy offered. "The pleasure is mine, young master C.J."

Craig turned and saw Danny standing by the edge of the driveway. He motioned him closer. His youngest held back a little, then walked toward them. Big eyes took in Jill's appearance, then lingered on the bright red car. Craig put down the suitcase and placed his hand on the boy's shoulder. Danny looked up at him and smiled.

Craig could go weeks without remembering, but sometimes, like now, when Danny smiled, it all came back. Krystal hadn't come home after she'd had their youngest. She'd sent a friend to pack up her clothes, and she'd walked away without looking back. Danny didn't know his mother, although he had some of her features. When the memories returned to force open old wounds, Craig clung to the only sane and constant source of strength in his world: his children.

He bent down and picked up Danny. The child placed one arm around his shoulder and leaned close. "She's pretty. The prettiest of all of them."

"Yes, she is," Craig answered softly. Jill was pretty. And sexy and all kinds of things that most men would enjoy. She was also his employee, and as that, she deserved his respect and nothing more.

C.J. was chattering on about the neighborhood, his friends and what he would really like her to serve for dinner. When his middle son started in on an earnest discussion of why it was important to have dessert with *every* meal, Craig interrupted.

"I'm sure Jill knows what to prepare, C.J."

The boy gave him an unrepentant grin. "Yeah, Dad, but a guy can always hope, can't he?"

"Sure. Hope all you want, then eat your vegetables. Jill, this is my youngest, Danny."

She moved close and touched the boy's arm. Her green eyes crinkled at the corners as she smiled. "Hi, Danny."

"Do you like little boys?" he asked. "Mrs. Greenway didn't. She said we were more trouble than we were worth."

Craig winced. Mrs. Greenway had stayed for three days before he'd fired her, but she'd made a lasting negative impression on the boys.

Jill nodded. "Of course I like little boys. What's not to like?" She glanced at Craig and rolled her eyes as if to ask what kind of person would take a job watching children if she didn't like them in the first place?

He opened his mouth to reply, then realized he had merely interpreted her look that way. She might have meant something else entirely. He'd barely known Jill Bradford an hour. They couldn't possibly be communicating that well.

But something bright and hot flared to life inside his chest. It wasn't about sex, although he still liked the way she looked in her jeans. It was something more dangerous. A flicker of interest in what and how a woman thought. As if they could be friends. As if he could trust her. Then he reminded himself he didn't trust anyone but family.

"Ben said you should get Mrs. Miller back," Danny said, his hold on Craig's shoulder tightening. "I miss her, too."

"Mrs. Miller was the boys' nanny for several years," Craig explained. "They miss her."

Danny looked at him and bit his bottom lip. "Do you think she misses us?"

"Of course. And now you have Jill."

"Until spring break," she reminded him.

"Until then," he agreed. Danny and C.J. both glanced at him. "Jill is taking the job temporarily. For five weeks. In the meantime, I'll find someone permanent."

Neither boy said anything. Craig fought back a feeling of frustration. How was he supposed to explain and make up for the ongoing turmoil in his children's lives? It would be different if they had the stability of two parents, but there was just him. He was doing the best he could, but sometimes, like now, he had the feeling it wasn't nearly enough.

"We've been alone for ten minutes, Dad," C.J. said. "We didn't burn the house down."

"Congratulations," Craig said. "As I told you before, my neighbor could only stay with them for an hour, so I really appreciate you coming back with me." He glanced at his watch. Damn. He was late already.

"I think your dad has to go to work. Why don't we go inside so he can show me everything, then be on his way?" Jill reached for Danny. Surprisingly, the boy let her lift him down. "You're heavy," she said admiringly. "You must be big for your age."

"He's a shorty," C.J. said, but his tone wasn't unkind.

"Am not!"

Jill bent down so she and Danny were at eye level. "I don't think you're short."

"That's 'coz you're shrimpy, too," he told her.

"Don't you know all the best things come in small packages?" They smiled at each other.

Craig picked up the suitcase again. "Lead the way," he said.

C.J. and Danny took off through the garage. Jill followed more slowly.

"I really appreciate you doing this," he said.

"I'm sure it will be fine." She spoke calmly, but when she glanced at him he could see the panic in her eyes. "It's just been a while since I was around kids."

"It's like riding a bike. You don't forget."

"Are you saying that because you're an expert?"

He paused in the middle of the garage. "No, because I'm a concerned father who's about to leave you alone with his three kids. I'm sort of hoping it's true so that everything will be okay."

"Don't worry. We'll survive."

"C.J. and Danny won't be much of a problem. They're easygoing, although some things still scare Danny."

"He's only six. What would you expect?"

"Exactly," he said, pleased that she was sympathetic. "Ben may not be so easy."

"He's the oldest?"

He nodded. "He's twelve."

"Does he get in a lot of trouble?"

"No. He doesn't do much of anything. He watches TV and plays video games." Craig didn't know what to do for his oldest. He didn't understand the boy's reluctance to participate in anything. Ben was the only one old enough to remember his mother. He didn't like to talk about it, but Craig knew he missed her. Maybe he even felt responsible for her leaving. But he'd never been able to get his son to talk about it.

Nothing had been normal since Krystal left. Not that it was so great before or that he'd ever once wanted her to come back. Hell, he didn't know what *was* normal anymore.

He turned around and pointed to the black sport-utility vehicle. "This is for you. You'll need it to take the boys places. C.J. plays several sports, and Danny is starting Pee-Wee league. The equipment fits in the back easily.''

"Groceries, too. I think all boys do is eat."

Craig didn't want to think about that. About Ben and how much weight he'd gained. "Yeah," he said. He walked toward the door leading into the house. "Here's the key." He touched a ring and key hanging from a hook on the wall. "It's an automatic, so you shouldn't have any trouble driving it."

She looked at the large truck-size vehicle. "As long as I don't have to parallel park, I'll be fine."

He opened the door and waited for her to step inside. She did so, then gasped audibly. He looked over her head and saw why.

There was a half bath on the right and the laundry room on the left. Piles of clothing toppled out of both rooms into the small hallway. More clothing was stacked in the family room. There were books, school backpacks, newspapers and toys littering the floor, coffee table and sofa. One end of the big dark blue leather sectional was buried under jackets and a pile of clean clothes he'd managed to run through the washer and dryer the previous evening. He'd asked the boys to sort out their belongings and take them upstairs, but no one had bothered.

Shoes formed an intricate pattern across the rug. Magazines for kids, car lovers, computer buffs and music fans had been tossed everywhere. Stacks of newspapers, more magazines, toys and a few actual books filled the bookcases on either side of the stone fireplace. The entertainment center to the right of the fireplace contained a TV, which was on, a VCR and stereo equipment. Videos had been piled next to the unit. The shelf where they belonged was bare.

Craig shifted her suitcase to his left hand and motioned to the mess. "I don't know what to say," he murmured. "I hadn't realized it had gotten so bad."

Jill turned and looked at him. Her green eyes were wide, her mouth open. "You didn't *realize?* How could you not? This isn't a mess it's a...a..." She closed her mouth. "I don't know what it is."

"I guess I should have gotten in a cleaning service."

He glanced around the room. C.J. and Danny were standing in front of the entrance to the kitchen. He was glad. If Jill saw that, she would turn tail and run. Damn it, he couldn't blame her, either. How had this happened? Why hadn't he been paying attention?

"There are four men living here," he said, by way of an explanation.

"More like four wild animals."

Danny chuckled at her comment. Jill smiled at the boy and the tightness at the base of Craig's neck eased a little. Maybe she wasn't going to leave.

"I'll get a service in," he said.

"I'll arrange it first thing Monday morning," she said, nudging a soccer ball out of her way so she could step farther into the room. "You don't want a nanny, Craig, you want a part-time slave. Anybody around here know what a vacuum looks like?"

"I do!" Danny said brightly. "But I've never used it."

"That seems to be a family trait."

Craig set the suitcase down. "I'm sorry, Jill. I should have noticed what had happened to this place. We haven't talked about salary yet and I—"

She held up her hand to stop him. "No. I can't be bribed. I agreed to do this for Kim and I will. For exactly what you were going to pay her. Just tell me one thing. Is it worse upstairs?"

"Sure is," C.J. said proudly and grinned. "Wanna see?"

"Not just yet."

Just then something moved on the sofa. Craig saw Ben stretching toward the remote control to change the channel. As always, the sight of his oldest brought on a wave of regret and frustration. He knew he was doing something wrong, but he didn't know what. He tried to encourage the boy to be more active. He practiced sports with him when he could. They'd talked about Ben needing to eat less. Nothing had helped. He could see his oldest was in a lot of pain, but he didn't know how to help.

"Ben, this is Jill Bradford."

Ben didn't bother turning his attention from the television. "I thought her name was Kim."

"I told you yesterday. Kim eloped. Jill is taking her place. Say hello."

"You're leaving us with someone you don't even know? A woman you've just met? Thanks, Dad."

The censure in the twelve-year-old's tone made Craig's hands tighten into fists, but he didn't move. He knew Ben was trying to get to him, but he wasn't going to let it happen. "Ms. Bradford isn't just some woman I found. I've interviewed her and checked on her. She's very—"

The sight of someone on the sofa had startled Jill enough that she was able to focus on something other than the disaster that had once been a very attractive family room. Craig's comment captured her attention. "You checked me out? Behind my back?"

"Yes." He frowned. "I don't know you. I can't trust my children with just anyone."

"I know but it's so yucky. Sneaking around behind my back."

"I did not *sneak.*"

His brown eyes darkened with a combination of concern and temper. She understood both. She shouldn't have questioned him, at least not in front of the boys. C.J. and Danny were staring at her, while Ben hadn't taken his attention from the television. The house looked as if it had been overrun by a fraternity, and she was about to be put in charge of three children. She who had sworn she would never get involved with someone else's kids again. She was in over her head and sinking fast. Yet she couldn't walk away. From the look of things, she was needed. Aaron, her ex-husband, had needed a wife and surrogate mother. Any woman would have done. These boys needed a nanny and there was no one else around. She'd always been a sucker for being needed. Only this time she was going to be smart. She was going to keep from getting personally involved. She wasn't the boys' part-time mother, and she wasn't Craig's part-time wife. She was only the hired help. Assuming she survived the first week, when spring break arrived she would be out of here. It was just a job.

Craig glanced at his watch again. He was obviously late. In his well-fitting black uniform, he looked competent and dangerous. An interesting combination. Her body continued to react to this close encounter with a good-looking man. She ignored the sweaty palms and slightly elevated pulse. He would be gone soon. From the looks of the house, he was gone a lot.

"I'll be fine," she said, stepping farther into the room. "You go to work. The boys and I will handle the introductions."

"Are you sure? I hate to leave you but I was due at the station a half hour ago."

"We have lots to do," she said, and smiled brightly. C.J. grinned in return. Danny gave her a shy half smile. Ben ignored everything but the television.

"Okay, boys, be good for Jill. If there's a problem, the station's number is by the phone in the kitchen. See ya." He gave a quick wave and disappeared out the door to the garage.

It was one of those moments when the television went perfectly silent. The sound of the closing door was unnaturally loud in the suddenly still room. Two pairs of eyes focused on her. Jill found herself fighting the urge to run out and tell Craig she'd changed her mind. Instead she glanced around the room, sure it couldn't be as bad as her first impression.

Nope. It was worse. It would take two days to get it picked up enough for the cleaning service to find the dirt. Dear Lord, what had she gotten into?

She thought briefly of Kim's now-empty house and where she was going to go when her roommate returned from her honeymoon. The last couple of nights alone had given her too much time to brood. She was beginning to see that she was coasting through life without any direction. It was time to get moving again. Maybe this challenge was just the jump start she needed.

"Okay, boys," she said. "Let's have a meeting and get to know each other. I want to hear how you do things, and I want to tell you what I expect in return."

Danny and C.J. were standing in front of the entrance to the kitchen. It was up two steps from the family room. The boys moved toward her. Jill stared at the kitchen and thought she might faint.

There wasn't a square inch of free counter space. Dishes, open boxes of cereal, empty containers of milk, cookies and bags of chips were everywhere. Cupboards were open; most of the shelves were bare. She thought of C.J.'s claim that upstairs was worse. She didn't want to know.

"Where are we going to have our meeting?" Danny asked.

She looked down at him. His light brown eyes were bright with questions and welcome. His shy smile was hard to resist. She glanced around to find a relatively clean spot. Through the kitchen she saw a formal dining room. The table didn't look too overrun with schoolbooks and sports equipment.

"In there," she said, pointing. "Come on, Ben."

The boy ignored her.

She walked over to stand in front of the TV. She was blocking the screen, but he continued to stare as if he could see the program.

"Don't you want to talk?" she asked.

"No. You're not going to stay, so why should I bother?"

"Because it's polite. The world is a nicer place when everyone tries to get along."

"You read that on a bumper sticker?" he asked rudely, still not looking at her.

"Oh, a smartmouth," she said. "Very nice. Very impressive. You think if you intimidate me, you get your way?"

He shrugged.

Ben had his father's dark hair. She suspected he had his eyes, too, but he wouldn't look at her so she couldn't tell. He was a good-looking kid, although about twenty pounds overweight.

From the corner of her eye, she saw C.J. and Danny watching. She hated being tested her first five minutes on the job and she hated it more that the other two brothers were here to witness the event. If she didn't get Ben's attention, the next five weeks were going to be miserable. She and Craig had given each other an out by agreeing to a one-week trial. If she really hated it here, she wouldn't mind leaving after that time, but she didn't want to be run off by a twelve-year-old with an attitude problem. She had her pride.

More than that, Ben reminded her of a growling but lonely dog. The animal desperately wants petting, but it's afraid to let anyone close enough. So instead, it scares the world away, then whimpers because it's alone.

Of course, she could be reading the situation completely wrong. After all, she'd had stepdaughters for nearly five years and had assumed they cared about her. She'd been proven wrong.

She spun around, then turned off the television. "Please come into the dining room, Ben."

She took a step away. Ben leaned forward and pressed a button on the remote control. The television popped back on. Defiance this soon wasn't good. Jill drew in a deep breath, not sure what to do. She and

Craig hadn't discussed discipline. Of course, there hadn't been time to discuss anything.

She thought about physically threatening Ben. There were two problems with that. First, it wasn't really her style. Second, she had a feeling he was taller than her. If only she knew what Craig did in situations like this. Then she looked around at the messy house and the three boys with emotionally hungry eyes. Maybe there wasn't a house rule. Maybe no one had the time or cared enough to lay down the law.

The problem with her trying to do it was that she didn't have a power base.

She could feel C.J. and Danny still watching her, waiting to see what she would do. This showdown with Ben was going to set the tone for her five weeks... or her one week, if she blew it.

Nothing like performing under pressure, she thought, staring at Ben and praying for inspiration. Like a gift from heaven, it arrived.

She smiled, then bent over and swept everything off the right half of the coffee table. Books, magazines, the television remote control, three glasses that were, fortunately, empty and plastic, and a half-eaten sandwich. Ben looked startled. Good. Better to keep him off-balance.

She knelt in front of the coffee table and placed her elbow on the slick wooden surface. She flexed and released her hand. "You ready to back up that smart mouth with some action?" she asked, trying to sound confident and tough. This was all going to blow up in her face if he beat her.

"What are you talking about?"

"You and me. Right here. Right now." She smiled. "Arm wrestling, Ben. If you win, you get to sit here

and watch TV until you're old and gray and your bones
are dissolving. If I win, you do what I say. Starting with
turning off the TV and coming with your brothers for
a meeting."

"Cool!" C.J. said. "You can beat him, Jill."

Ben glared at his brother. "This is stupid," he muttered.

But he wasn't looking at the television anymore, Jill
thought triumphantly. She shrugged. "Maybe. If
you're chicken."

"I'm *not* chicken."

Danny made a clucking noise.

"Shut up, brat."

"I'm not a brat."

"You're a shrimpy brat."

"Boys." Jill spoke firmly. Both of them looked at
her. She stared at Ben. "Put up or shut up, young man.
Either you're tough, or you're not. Let's find out."

Those dark eyes stared at her. She tried to figure out
what he was thinking, but along with his father's good
looks, Ben had inherited Craig's ability to keep some
of his thoughts to himself.

"If I win, I get to watch TV and I get five bucks."

She thought for a moment, then nodded slowly. "If
*I* win, you not only do what I say, but you give up TV
for the weekend."

Ben glanced at her right arm, then at her. "Deal."
He slid off the sofa and onto the carpet. After placing
his elbow on the coffee table, he clasped her hand with
his. C.J. and Danny moved closer.

"Come on, Jill, you can do it," Danny said loudly.
He ignored Ben's glare.

Jill hoped the boy's confidence in her was going to
pay off. Since moving in with Kim, she'd started

working out with light weights. She knew she was stronger than she had been, but was it enough? She knew very little about the strength of twelve-year-old boys. She could only hope that Ben's inactive life-style gave her an advantage.

Her gaze locked with Ben's. A flicker of uncertainty flashed through his eyes. She thought he might be a little afraid of winning. That would give him more power than most children would find comfortable. At least she liked to think so.

"C.J., you say go," she said, and shifted on the carpet. Ben would probably go for the quick kill. If she could hold on during that, she might have a chance. If she could win, she would make it look hard, so Ben could save face.

Ah, the complications of dealing with a houseful of men, she thought. She leaned forward so she could have the maximum leverage and sucked in a breath.

"Go!" C.J. yelled.

## Chapter Three

Jill thought she'd prepared herself for the assault, but when it came, Ben nearly drove her hand into the table. She managed to keep him from slamming it down, but barely. She had to bite her lip to keep from crying out.

She didn't look at him or either of the other boys. She focused all her attention on her arm, willing it to be strong.

She finally managed to get their hands back in an upright position. She pressed hard, and he gave. She risked glancing at him. She saw the panic on his face. He was about to be humiliated in front of his brothers.

Her heart went out to this stubborn, proud, overweight boy who probably endured the taunts of his classmates and the lack of confidence that went with not fitting in. She was torn between wanting to make him feel better and needing to establish a presence in the house. As she'd decided, if she could win, she would. But she wouldn't make it look easy.

Her arm was shaking, but not as badly as Ben's. They knelt there, with their arms perpendicular to the table.

"You gonna beat 'im, Jill?" Danny asked, earning a glare from his oldest brother.

"I'm trying," she said through gritted teeth. She moved slightly to the left, forcing his wrist down.

C.J. laughed. "Come on, Ben. She's just a girl."

"Then you try it," Ben complained. "She's stronger than she looks."

"Lesson number one," Jill said. "Never underestimate the power of a woman."

With that she pressed the back of his hand down onto the wood. Both C.J. and Danny cheered. Ben released her fingers and rubbed his wrist as if it hurt.

"I thought I'd win for sure," he said, then smiled sheepishly. In that moment, he looked exactly like his father. He was going to be a heartbreaker when he grew up, she thought. He leaned over, grabbed the remote control, turned off the television, then handed the clicker to her.

"Haynes men keep their word," he said simply.

He sounded so serious. The words were those of a mature man, not a twelve-year-old boy. But the way he said them, she believed him.

"You're being very gracious," she said. She was surprised. She'd thought he would be a sore loser. One point for him, she thought, deciding that if he really cooperated with her today, she would let him watch a little TV tonight. She'd learned early on it paid to compromise.

"Okay, why don't the three of you give me the nickel tour."

Danny frowned. "We get a nickel if we give you a tour?"

"No, stupid. It's just an expression."

Apparently Ben's magnanimous attitude didn't extend to his brothers. "No name-calling, please." She stood up and placed her hand on Danny's shoulder. "But Ben is right. 'Nickel tour' is just an expression. It means to give someone a quick tour. Not a lot of details."

"Oh, okay."

C.J. looked at her and grinned. "Are you sure you want to see the rest of the house?"

She glanced at the piles of laundry by the door to the garage, then at the dishes in the kitchen. "Sure. How bad can it be?"

The three boys laughed together.

Fifteen minutes later, Jill didn't feel like laughing. She wanted to turn tail and run. She didn't understand how people could live under these conditions. It didn't make sense. Didn't anyone notice that virtually every possession was out of the cupboards, closets and drawers and on the floor?

She stood in the center of the upstairs hall, staring at C.J.'s room. "Doesn't your dad make you pick up your stuff?" she asked.

"Oh, sure," he told her. "All the time. He gets real mad if we don't."

"Then explain this." She motioned to the toys, books, clothes and cassette tapes littering the room.

"He's been gone." C.J. gave her a charming smile. All three brothers were going to cut a swath through the female population when they got older. But for now they were just messy little boys.

There were four bedrooms upstairs. To the left was Craig's. Not wanting to pry, she'd only peeked inside. She'd had a brief impression of large pieces of furniture and a bed that looked big enough to sleep six. Of course, she wasn't even five foot two. To Craig the bed was probably just big enough. His room was relatively tidy, with only a few pieces of clothing tossed on the sofa facing the corner fireplace.

Next to his bedroom was a small alcove. There was a large desk with a computer and printer. Disks had been piled around the keyboard. On the wall was a bulletin board covered with computer-generated graphics.

Each boy had his own bedroom. First Danny's, then C.J.'s, then Ben's. The bathroom they shared was right next to the stairs. Jill glanced in each of the rooms and saw far more than she wanted to. Danny had toys piled everywhere, C.J. had tons of clothes scattered and Ben seemed to be storing half the plates and glasses on his floor. Aside from that, the three rooms were all identical, each with a twin bed, a dresser, a desk and a set of bookshelves attached to the wall.

"You're all slobs," she said, pausing outside their bathroom door. It was closed. She thought about opening it and looking inside, but then decided that some things were best left for professionals.

"We work hard at it," C.J. said.

Danny moved next to her and touched her hand. "I'll help you clean up."

"Thanks, honey."

Ben snorted. "The little shrimp's already sucking up."

"Am not!"

"Are too!"

"Excuse me," Jill said loudly. "You're all going to help me clean up. We're going to do the laundry, pick up everything that doesn't belong on the floor and do the dishes."

There was a collective groan.

"I'm sorry," Jill said. "But it's your fault. If you'd chosen to live like civilized people instead of baboons—"

She knew the word was a mistake as soon as she said it. Instantly all three boys hunched over and started making monkey noises.

"Herds of the Serengeti, return to the family room," she said over the din of their hooting.

They began the awkward shuffle down the stairs. Halfway there, the game changed and became a race. The in-line skates resting on the foyer floor created a hazard, but everyone avoided them.

"Where does the sports equipment go?" she asked.

"There's a closet under the stairs," C.J. told her.

She found the door and opened it. The storage space had a slanted ceiling, but the floor space of a small room. It was empty. "Ah, I see you like to keep it clean in here and not in the rest of the house. It makes perfect sense now. Why didn't someone tell me?"

C.J. grinned, Danny giggled, even Ben forgot to scowl. Together, the four of them walked into the family room. Jill saw her suitcase sitting there. "Where do I sleep?" she asked, realizing she hadn't seen a guest room.

"Here," Danny said, pointing to a door at the far end of the family room.

She walked around him and stuck her head inside the cheerful bedroom. Big windows looked out onto the backyard. The white wicker furniture looked new. There was a bright yellow bedspread on the double bed, and she could see the entrance to her own private bath.

This was by far the cleanest part of the house.

"Dad says we're not allowed in here," Danny said. "Mrs. Miller lived here before she had to go away. Now you live here."

Jill thought about pointing out the fact that her stay was temporary but figured the boys had been through enough today. Instead, she carried her suitcase into her room, then tried to figure out what should be done first.

"Danny and C.J., you two start sorting laundry."

The boys stared at her blankly, identically confused expressions drawing their mouths into straight lines.

"Clothes," she said, pointing to the piles around the laundry room and flowing into the hallway. "Sort them. By color. One pile for whites. One pile for darks, one for lights and another for jeans."

A lock of medium brown hair fell across Danny's forehead. He was the only one of the Haynes males she'd seen who didn't have dark hair and eyes. "Those piles are going to be huge. They're going to reach the ceiling."

She looked at the mounds of clothing. "Oh, probably, but do the best you can. Ben, I'd like you to help me in the kitchen. We're going to load the dishwasher and try to figure out what color the counters are."

"I know what color they are," C.J. said. "They're white."

She leaned over and wrapped an arm around his neck. Rubbing her knuckles against the top of his head, she said, "I *know* they're white. I was just being funny."

The boy giggled and wiggled, but didn't move away. Her chest tightened in sympathy as she wondered when they had last been hugged by a woman. It couldn't be easy growing up without a mom.

She released C.J. He and Danny went to work on the clothes. Ben followed her into the kitchen, and with only minor grumbling began loading the dishwasher. Jill sorted through cereal boxes, figuring out which were empty and which just needed to be put away. There were piles of food. Bread, chips, jars of salsa. A melted carton of ice cream had spilled on, then stuck to, the counter. She wet a cloth and set it over the mess. Maybe by that night it would have loosened up a little.

From the family room came muffled sounds of a battle being waged. C.J. and Danny were tossing more clothes than they were piling, but the work was getting done. Ben made the flatware dive-bomb the dishwasher. The childish sounds brought back memories of being with her two stepdaughters. She shoved the last box of cereal onto the top pantry shelf and wondered what they were doing now. Did they ever think of her or miss her? She still remembered how hard it had been to lose them. Even after her divorce from Aaron, she'd wanted to see the girls. She'd tried to call them, but their mother said to leave them alone. Jill had quickly found out she didn't have any legal rights to visitation, and when she'd pushed the matter, Patti and Heather had phoned her directly and told her to stop bothering them. They had a mother, they didn't need her.

The words still had the power to wound her. She hadn't tried to take their mother's place in their lives. She'd just wanted to love them. Was that so bad? It must be a horrible crime because they'd never forgiven her for it.

"You got a husband?" Ben asked.

She spun toward him. He was stacking plates in the bottom of the dishwasher and had his back to her. "No. I'm not married."

"Got any kids?"

"No. Of course not. If I had children, I would be with them."

He looked up at her. "Why?"

"I just would. I wouldn't—" She had started to say, "leave my children," but clamped her mouth shut. Craig had told her that the boys' mother had left them.

Without thinking, she crossed the room to stand next to him. She reached out to touch him, then had second thoughts. Her hand hung awkwardly between them. At the same moment she moved closer, he started to straighten. A lock of dark hair fell onto his forehead. She reached up and brushed it back. Ben stiffened, but didn't move away.

She smiled, then frowned. She was looking *up*. "My word, you *are* taller than me!"

He grinned. Once again, he reminded her of his father. If he could just lose a little weight, he would be a good-looking kid. She wondered what Craig would think if she tried to help Ben with his problem.

By the time Ben had filled the dishwasher and stacked up the dishes for the next load, she'd found out there was no fresh food in the house. Actually there was very little to eat at all. When she commented on the fact, Ben told her that his father had meant to go shopping that day, but he'd been called to work.

"He's on some secret assignment," he said. "He can't talk about it."

"You must be very proud of him. Not many people get to make a difference every time they go to work."

Ben seemed startled by her compliment, then he smiled slowly. "Yeah, I am proud of my dad." Then the smile faded. Was he thinking of all the times his dad was gone?

"I don't suppose he mentioned when he'd be home," she said.

Ben shook his head. "There's phone numbers on the wall." He pointed to a bulletin board stuck above the telephone.

Jill walked over and stared at them. There was the number for the police station, a doctor, then a list of men. Travis, Jordan, Kyle and Austin.

"They're my uncles," Ben offered. "Except Austin. He's not really, but we call him Uncle because we've known him forever."

It must be nice, she thought, thinking of her own scattered family. She'd been an only child and her parents had split up while she was still in grade school. She'd spent the next seven years being shuffled between one household and the other, never really feeling settled or wanted in either.

"We're done!" Danny announced.

She looked into the family room and saw four mountains of laundry. "That's got to be twenty loads," she said in awe.

"It'll take forever," Danny said.

"Maybe not forever. Maybe just until you're in college."

He giggled at the thought.

She made the boys soup and sandwiches for lunch. There was just enough food to get them through the day. She didn't want to go grocery shopping without talking to Craig and finding out what her budget was. While the boys ate, she put in the first load of whites.

"I can do it loud," C.J. said, then slurped his soup.

"That's nothing," Ben said, and proceeded to prove his point.

There was laughter and more slurping. She bit back a smile. These boys were different from her step-daughters, but she liked them. They were alive and made her feel the same way. That was something she hadn't enjoyed in a long time.

After a few minutes, the slurping became annoying. She didn't want to tell them to just stop. Better to condition them into following the rules. Easier for everyone in the long run.

"Are you three having a slurping contest?" she asked as she closed the laundry room door behind her.

"I'm winning," Danny said.

"Are you? Oh, that's too bad. Whoever comes in last gets the largest serving of ice cream for dessert."

Silence descended like night at the equator. Instantly and irrevocably. She had to fight back her smile. Ah, the power of dessert. It was a lesson she'd learned well. There was one last carton in the freezer, so she could make good on her promise. She looked at Ben and thought it might be better to get low-fat frozen yogurt next time.

C.J. glanced up at her. "You tricked us, Jill."

"I know." This time she allowed herself to grin. "Being a grown-up is pretty cool."

It was nearly midnight when Craig opened the front door and stepped into the house. Jill's car was still in the driveway. He'd forgotten to give her the garage door opener so she could park her Mustang inside.

He'd also forgotten to discuss the details of her salary, give her money for food or talk about days off. He'd left in a hurry because he'd been late. And because he'd been afraid she would change her mind about taking care of the boys. Frankly, he couldn't have blamed her.

He closed the door behind him. There was a nightlight at the top of the stairs, and the house was quiet. Everyone had survived. Relief swept over him, and with it, guilt. Just because he didn't know what to do about his boys didn't mean he could avoid them. He had to take responsibility. Sometimes, though, it was hard being the only one they could depend on.

He glanced at the living room, then did a double take. Where there had been piles of junk sat only furniture. The dining room was the same. He moved to his right, down the small open hall and glanced into the kitchen. The counters were clear, the sink clean, the trash can empty. Beyond, in the family room, most of the toys and sports equipment had been picked up. The videotapes were off the floor and the few piles of laundry left had been sorted by color.

He moved farther into the room. The TV was off, but lights were on. Jill lay curled up asleep at one end of the sofa. All around her were piles of clean, folded laundry. He didn't know whether to wake her up or leave her in peace. He'd never thought of the sofa as particularly comfy, but she was a lot smaller than he.

Before he could decide, she turned her head toward him and opened her eyes. The bright green color surprised him. He'd forgotten the intensity of her gaze. Then she smiled. His body reacted with all the subtlety of a freight train crashing into a brick wall. Blood flowed hot and fast. His breathing increased and an almost unfamiliar pressure swelled in his groin.

"You're home," she said, her voice low and husky. "I wondered if you would be. I almost called the station, but I didn't want to bother you. Is everything okay?"

"Fine." He motioned to the folded laundry. "I'm sorry. I didn't mean to make you do all this work. I really was going to call a service."

"You still are." She sat up and stretched. The hem of her sweatshirt rode up, exposing the barest sliver of bare belly before descending and hiding all from view. "I don't mind doing the laundry and cooking, but I'm scared to go into the boys' bathroom. I think they've invented some new fungus, and I don't want to have to battle it."

"I'll call on Monday," he promised.

She shifted so she was leaning against the arm of the sofa and rested her chin on the back. "I already did. They'll be here at ten. Are you hungry?"

His stomach rumbled at the question. "I guess I am. Come to think of it, I didn't have time to eat today."

She rose to her feet. She must have been asleep for a while. Her hair was all spiky, and it reminded him of their encounter that morning. When she'd been in her robe... and nothing else.

The mental image did nothing to alleviate his now-painful condition. Nor did he want it to. It had been far too long since he'd desired a woman. He didn't have to do anything about it with Jill. In a way it was enough to still be able to feel something.

"Don't be too impressed," she said, leading the way into the kitchen. "It's just pizza. There isn't much here, but I didn't want to go grocery shopping without talking to you first."

"I'm sorry about that, too. I just took off and dumped everything on you. I'd meant to discuss some things, but I had to go in and..." He gave her a half-hearted smile and rubbed the back of his neck. The pain there was pretty constant, the sort of nagging ache brought on by too much stress and too little of everything else.

"Don't worry about it," she said. She opened a box on the counter and slid three slices of thin-crust pizza with everything onto a plate. Then she put it into the microwave oven to heat and opened the refrigerator. "Water, milk, soda or beer?"

"Beer."

She took the bottle and untwisted the cap. "Have a seat," she said, handing him the drink and motioning to the kitchen table. She poured a glass of water for herself.

He stared at it for a moment. "I'm trying to remember the last time I saw this kitchen so clean."

"Judging from the number of dishes we put through the dishwasher, I would say some time last Christmas." She held up her hand before he could speak. "Don't apologize again. I understand. But we do have a few details to work out."

He settled in the seat at the head of the table and gratefully drank his beer. She pulled the pizza out of the oven and gave it to him, then took the chair opposite his. While he ate, they discussed her salary, the grocery budget, the kids' schedules for school and sports.

"Danny and C.J. need to be picked up but Ben takes the bus," he said, then bit into the third piece of pizza.

She sat cross-legged on the kitchen chair. Just looking at her folded legs made his knees throb. She'd run her hands through her hair, but there were still spiky tufts sticking up. Most of the lights in the house were off. Only the lamp in the family room and a small light over the stove illuminated the kitchen. In the dim room, her pupils were huge, nearly covering her irises, and her eyes looked black against her pale skin.

Her small hands fluttered gracefully as she moved. She made notes on a yellow pad, detailing where to pick up whom and what foods made the boys gag.

"I'm not a fancy cook, but pretty much everything I put together is edible," she said.

"That's all we require."

She glanced at him. "This has been hard on you, hasn't it?"

"Yeah." He took a swallow of beer and set the bottle on the table. "Since Mrs. Miller left there's been four different women in here. I guess she spoiled us. I didn't think it would be that difficult to replace her, but I was wrong."

"Well, you've got another five weeks until you have to think about that."

He raised his eyebrows. "What happened to our one-week trial?"

She shrugged. "I spent the day with the boys, and I think I can handle it. Unless they don't like me, I can't think of a reason why I can't stay the agreed time. At least it will save you from having to look for someone instantly."

"I think I've interviewed nearly every nanny in a fifty-mile radius."

He supposed he could have put the boys in some kind of day-care program and then just hired sitters for the weekends, but that never seemed to work out. He had to coordinate meals, cleaning, food shopping. It was easier to find one person to do it all. He was fortunate enough to have the money to pay for outside help. Every day he saw people who survived on much less.

"Now you get a break," Jill said. "Besides, staying here gives me some time, too. When Kim and her husband come home from their honeymoon, the last thing they'll want is a houseguest. I was going to have to look for my own place anyway. I haven't decided if I want to stay here or go back to San Clemente." She looked at him and smiled. "Now I don't have to."

Intellectually he knew his boys were sleeping upstairs. There were neighbors across the street and next door. He and Jill were hardly alone. Yet he couldn't shake the feeling of the world having been reduced to just the two of them. In the brief silences of their conversation he could hear the soft sound of her breathing. Despite his best effort to keep his attention above her shoulders, his gaze was drawn again and again to her chest. Not just to stare at her breasts, although they stirred his imagination, but also to watch her breathe. She wasn't like any woman he'd ever dated. Of course, he was getting old and there was a chance he couldn't remember back that far.

He studied her hands on the glass. Her slender fingers made random patterns in the condensation. Her nails were short and unpainted, but still feminine. He couldn't get over how small she was, every part of her perfectly proportioned, but little. Krystal had been tall, nearly five-nine. Most of the women he'd dated had been tall, as well.

"I didn't know how you wanted to handle discipline with the boys," she said.

"Ben's already been a problem?"

She raised her eyebrows. "Why assume it was him?"

"C.J. is very charming and fun-loving. Like my brother Kyle. He prefers to get his way by cajoling. Danny is going to be shy for the first couple of days, which leaves only Ben."

Ben had also been a problem in the past. Craig grimaced as he remembered the reports from Ben's teachers. The boy was sullen and uncooperative. His grades continued to be good, but he didn't participate in group activities.

"I did convince him to behave," she said, then stared down at the table. "But I'm not sure you'll approve of the method." She glanced up, her gaze sheepish. "I didn't know if you did time-outs or sent the boys to their rooms, and I was afraid if I demanded he do something, he wouldn't. He's even taller than me."

"So what did you do?"

"I challenged him to an arm-wrestling match. If I won, he had to do what I said. If he won, he got to watch TV for the rest of the weekend." She paused and took a sip of water. "I don't know if it's right or not, but when kids get old enough, I like to work out a compromise with them. Time-outs, then removing privileges. I make deals, because that's a part of life. No one gets everything all the time."

He was intrigued. And impressed. "Did you win?"

She smiled slowly. "Yes, but at first I was afraid I wasn't going to. For what it's worth, he was a very gracious loser."

"That's something." The pain at the back of his neck got worse. He rubbed it, wondering when it was going to go away. Probably about the time he got his life together. Like in the next century or so.

"What's wrong?" she asked.

"Nothing. Just stress."

"Do you want some aspirin?"

"That would be great."

She walked across the family room and into her bedroom. When she returned carrying two pills in the palm of her hand, he felt another flash of pain that had nothing to do with the tightness of his muscles. This one involved his soul.

He missed being a part of someone's life. He missed the day-to-day sameness of married life. He didn't miss being married to Krystal, but he missed being emotionally committed to a woman.

He looked at Jill, at her pert features and her bright green eyes. She smiled as she handed over the medication. Their hands barely touched, yet he felt the jolt all the way to his groin.

He'd hired Jill for the boys, to make their lives stable. He hadn't known inviting her into his home was going to cause him to want all the things he knew he could never have.

## Chapter Four

"How was your day?" Jill asked as Craig took the aspirin and swallowed.

He hesitated, not sure how to answer her question. A lot of his special project was confidential. Before he could decide what to tell her, she settled in the seat opposite him and wrinkled her nose.

"Don't worry about it," she said briskly. "I understand you're involved in something secret. I wasn't asking to get privileged information, I was just being polite. You know. How was your day? My day was fine. That sort of thing."

She tugged on a sleeve of her sweatshirt, pulling the cuff until it was up near her elbow. As she repeated the procedure on her other arm, he noticed how small and delicate her wrists were.

"I'm not used to someone asking," he said at last, mostly because it was the truth. Lately no one had been around enough to bother. He leaned back in his chair and studied the bottle of beer in front of him. "It was ... difficult. Every time I think I'm immune to the scum of the world, they manage to surprise me."

She scooted forward and rested her elbows on the table. "What are they doing now?"

"I can't talk about the specifics of the case, but I'll tell you what was reported in the press." He grimaced. "Not on the front page, of course. Someone ripping off the elderly isn't exciting enough."

"Is that what's going on?"

"Yeah. There's a ring of three, maybe four people who get in accidents with senior drivers. They'll stop suddenly so they get rear-ended, or they turn left on a yellow light and drive slow enough to get hit. Anything to make the victims think the accident is their fault. Then they pretend to be concerned, talking about how an aging parent lost his or her license because of an accident. They mention increased insurance rates. It's based on truth, which makes it more frightening for the victims. Often they convince the senior drivers to pay in cash for damages to the car."

"The price of which is several times what it's supposed to be, right?" Jill asked, her green eyes flashing with anger. "How horrible. I don't understand people like that. It's cruel and ugly. I'm glad you're doing something to stop them."

Craig stared at her, surprised by the vehemence of her reaction. Sometimes he talked to his brothers about his work. Except for Jordan, they were cops and they understood. Krystal never had. When he'd tried to talk about his work, she'd gotten bored. In her opinion the fools of the world got what they deserved.

Now, with the perfect vision of hindsight, he wondered what he'd ever seen in her. But he already knew the answer to that question. At twenty-two she'd been stunningly beautiful with a body that could tempt a saint. She knew how to use her best assets to her advantage, and for some reason, she'd set her sights on him. He hadn't been thinking with his head when he'd proposed. The worst of it was, he couldn't even regret what had happened between them. Marrying Krystal had been a mistake, but he would do it all over again if given the choice. The reward of his children wasn't something he could wish away.

"It's slow going," he said, and shrugged. "I'm working with a team of elderly citizens. We're mounting a sting operation."

She grinned. "I bet they're great to work with."

"They are," he agreed. "There's this one woman, Mrs. Hart. She lives alone. She's got to be seventy, but you'd never know it. She's been begging me to let her wear a wire." He glanced at Jill. "A microphone and tape. She keeps cruising around the seniors center and the bingo halls, hoping they'll pick her. I keep telling her she's seen too many movies."

"She sounds terrific."

"Yeah." His smile faded and he hunched over his beer. "I hope they don't get her. A couple of the accidents didn't go as planned. The timing was off, or the jerks doing this stopped too soon. A woman was killed."

"Oh, Craig." She reached across the table and touched his hand with her fingers. The light brush wasn't erotic. Nor was it meant to be. Instead, the caring gesture offered comfort and he accepted it.

"We'll get 'em. I don't usually do this kind of work, but the detectives needed some assistance and I volunteered. When the hours keep me away from the kids, I try to justify it by telling myself I'm doing the right thing."

"You are," she assured him. She pulled her hand away and laced her fingers together on the edge of the table. "Why a cop?"

"That's easy. I come from a long line of cops. Four generations on my dad's side. All my uncles—my dad was one of six. Two of my brothers. Jordan's the only holdout. He's a fire fighter. We tease him about it." Craig took a sip of beer. "If you ask me, anyone voluntarily going into a burning building day after day is crazy."

"Some people would say that about what you do."

"Maybe."

The corners of her mouth tilted up. "So you're one of four boys, you have five uncles and three boys of your own. There aren't many girls in your family, are there?"

"There hadn't been one born in four generations. My brother Travis had a girl, though."

"Oh, progress for the female gender."

"Jordan has a theory that Haynes men only have girls when they're in love. If it's true, it doesn't say much about the last four generations of husbands. Or my marriage. Elizabeth—that's Travis's wife—says it's more about the female being predisposed to accept male or female sperm. She pointed out that she's one of three girls, and she comes from a family that mostly has daughters. I guess when Kyle and Sandy have their baby we'll know who's right."

Jill was staring at him as if he'd grown a second head. "You look lost," he said.

"I am. All these names. How big is your family?"

"I have three brothers and Austin. He's family, but not by blood."

"Where are your folks?"

He didn't like talking about that, but it was a reasonable question. "My mom took off about fifteen years ago. My dad hadn't been much of a husband. He fooled around constantly. She took it for as long as she could, then one day she walked out. She didn't bother packing a bag or leaving a note. She just left. We never saw her again."

"If she didn't take any luggage, how do you know—" She bit on her lower lip.

"How do we know something didn't happen to her?"

She nodded.

"Jordan saw her leave. She told him she'd had it and wasn't coming back. He was only seventeen and didn't know what to do. He came to me. I was already out of college and living on my own. I told him to keep what he heard to himself. It was hard on all of us. Probably hardest on Kyle, because he's the youngest."

Her green eyes were wide and dark with emotion. It wasn't pity. Maybe concern. "I'm sorry."

"Thanks. My brothers and I were always close, but after that, we pulled together more. My dad remarried a couple of times, then moved to Florida. I haven't seen him since before Ben was born." And he didn't want to. He would never forgive his father for what he'd done to the family.

"You'll meet my brothers while you're here," he said. "We get together a lot."

"It sounds nice, but a little overwhelming. I'm an only child. As it is, I'm going to have my hands full adjusting to living with a houseful of men." She grinned. "I'm thrilled to have my own bathroom so I won't have to fight to keep the toilet seat down."

"I trained them better than that. It shouldn't be a problem anywhere."

She looked at the table, then at him. Her full mouth straightened. "You know, Craig, despite how you're beating yourself up right now, you've done a good job with the boys."

"I don't think I want to know how you read my mind."

"It wasn't hard. I think most single parents worry that they're not doing enough. Add to that the pressures that go with your job and it doesn't take a rocket scientist to figure it out. But from what I saw today, they're good kids."

"I can't take credit for that," he said. "Everything is so messed up." Ben. What was he going to do about his oldest?

"Divorce has a way of doing that to families."

He took a swallow of beer. "So what's your story?"

"It's not very interesting." She leaned back in her chair and raised her hands, palms up. "I met a man I loved and who I thought loved me. It was a whirlwind courtship. I married him, and his two daughters came to live with us." She smiled, but there was sadness in her eyes.

"Patti and Heather were so sweet. I adored them. I wanted to be their mother. I did everything I could for them. I was working, so I didn't have a lot of time." She paused, as if thinking. "I was working extra hours. Aaron had high alimony payments so I supported the household. I really didn't mind. Looking back, I suppose I should have.''

"How long has it been?"

"Eighteen months. I know what you're thinking. That I should be over it by now. In a way I am. It's just that I tried too hard not to think about it, and then one day I couldn't think about anything else.''

"I'm surprised Aaron allowed you to support his two kids." He shook his head. "I guess I shouldn't be. My ex-wife used to tell me that I was old-fashioned. According to her, my philosophies about men and women went out with hoopskirts.''

"We never really talked about it," she said. "I sort of offered and he accepted. It was an unspoken rule in our family. He didn't have to say what he wanted or needed. I just knew.''

Craig understood about that kind of selfishness. He'd grown up watching his father expect the same from his mother. "But he never bothered figuring out what you wanted.''

She shook her head. "The really sad part is, until a few months ago, I had convinced myself I didn't want anything at all. That just being part of the family was enough.''

He and Krystal had been the same way, except in his case, he'd been the one anticipating her needs. She'd taken easily, without once feeling the need to give back. As a point of honor, he'd done the opposite of his father. He'd sworn fidelity. Foolishly, he'd expected the same. But Krystal had never agreed with him about that. In fact, they'd agreed on very little.

Jill drew in a slow breath. "Eventually I figured out Aaron married me to get custody of the children. It hurt, but I got over it. Then one day we ended up in court.''

She drew her knees to her chest and wrapped her arms around her calves. He wanted to move around the table and comfort her. The impulse surprised him. He'd known this woman less than twenty-four hours. Yet there was something about the night. Something about the moment and the confessions that made it seem that they'd known each other for much longer. Maybe it was the shared pain. Like wounded warriors, they talked about their injuries and knew what the other had endured.

''His ex-wife won back custody of her daughters and just like that the girls were gone.'' She blinked several times. ''Then Aaron didn't need me anymore.''

Everything about her—the way her shoulders hunched forward, the set of her mouth, her fingers locked so tightly together that her knuckles turned white—told him there was more to the story. But he didn't ask.

She looked up and forced a shaky smile. ''I tell myself it's Aaron's loss. I doubt I was the best wife in the world, but I tried hard, and I make a dynamite meat loaf. How many people can claim that kind of f-fame?'' Her voice cracked on the last word.

She cleared her throat and continued. ''I could have handled it,'' she said softly. ''If only someone had told me it was just temporary. I wouldn't have felt like such a fool. I would have made sure it wouldn't hurt so bad.''

''Your ex-husband and my ex-wife should be locked up together. They deserve each other.''

She glanced at him. ''I thought you said Krystal was, ah, you know.''

"Dead?"

She nodded.

"She is. But they still deserve each other. Aaron sounds like a jerk."

"Don't expect me to defend him," she said. "I'm done with that. And while I appreciate the words of support, I'd like to remind you that you've known me a day. You've only heard my side of this story. His is probably completely different."

"Maybe, but I'll take your word for what really happened. I'm sure Aaron regrets the loss. You've got a lot going for you."

She chuckled. "Oh, sure. I have a temporary job, after which I'll be unemployed again. I'm divorced and just turned thirty. Men are lining up for miles."

He wanted to tell her he would line up, but that would lead them in a direction neither of them wanted to go. Even as he held back the words, he noticed how the soft light cast shadows on her face, highlighting her cheekbones. In his mind, she *did* have a lot going for her. She was bright, funny and sexy as hell. And small. Concern mixed with desire as he wondered if he would physically hurt her if they ever . . .

He cut off that line of thought. They weren't ever going to do anything. They'd both learned their lessons.

"You've probably been wondering why I'm living with Kim," she said. "I do plan to get back to my life. I did fine for just over a year. I grieved, I got angry, I did all the things those self-help books say you're supposed to. I moved on. Then one day I couldn't do anything but feel the pain. The thought of going to my job overwhelmed me. I realized that instead of actually going through the steps, I'd been talking about them and thinking about them, but not being in them, if that makes sense. Circling around them like a caged lion. I needed to get away and start over. Kim had lost her roommate so moving in with her seemed like the perfect thing to do. I leased out my condo and drove up.''

She rested her chin on her knees. ''You know what hurts the most?''

''No.''

''I don't miss Aaron so much. I miss those girls. That was the worst. Finding out they'd been using me, too. Apparently they'd been calling their mother all the time and I never knew. She was telling them things about me. Mean things. I thought they cared about me and they didn't.'' Her voice got thick. She swallowed.

''In court—'' She cleared her throat, obviously fighting tears. ''In court, when we lost custody, I asked if I could see them sometime. The judge told me I had no legal rights. Then he asked the girls what they wanted. They laughed at me and made fun of me. I had no idea. I—''

He hadn't meant to go to her, but he couldn't watch her in pain anymore. He rose from his chair and circled the table. Before she could protest, he picked her up in his arms. She didn't weigh as much as Ben, he thought, surprised. She murmured a protest, but he ignored her and settled on her seat, with her on his lap.

She was as tiny as he'd imagined she would be, with slim arms, slender legs and small hands. She tried to push away.

''Damn it, Jill, I'm not making a pass at you,'' he said. ''I'm giving you a hug.''

''I know, but this—'' Then a tear escaped from her right eye. She brushed it away and buried her face in his shoulder.

She didn't cry. She just huddled against him, shaking with misery. Her ragged breathing fanned his neck. He told himself it wasn't about sex, and despite the arousal pressing against his fly, it wasn't. She needed holding, and he needed to hold.

Craig tried to remember the last time he'd been this close to a woman. He tried to remember the last time he'd wanted to be.

He inhaled the sweet fragrance of Jill's body. He stroked his hands up and down her back. Bits of what she'd told him floated through his mind. He wanted to find her ex-husband and beat him into a bloody pulp. He wanted to talk some sense into those two girls. He worked with the worst type of humanity every day, but he hated to see others tainted and hurt by contamination.

"Damn," she said, and straightened. Her face was dry, her mouth pulled into a straight line. "This is horribly unprofessional behavior. I swear, I don't usually fall apart like this."

"It's okay."

"No, it's not. But thanks for pretending. You're a nice man."

She sniffed once, then slid off his lap. He let her go, because he had no excuse to keep her, and trying to make one up would be dangerous for both of them. At this moment, with his groin swollen and aching and his blood pounding through his heated body, he didn't feel very nice.

She brushed her cheek with the back of her hand, then smiled. If the corners trembled a little, he wasn't going to mention it.

"Bet you're sorry you asked about *my* life," she said.

"Actually, I'm not."

"It's probably better that you know. I'll do a good job with your kids, but I won't get personally involved. In five weeks I'm going to walk away. I can't risk getting hurt again."

"I understand."

"Thanks for everything. Good night."

She gave him a brief wave, then walked down the two stairs into the family room, and across to her bedroom. She closed the door behind her.

He watched her go, then stood alone in the silence. He couldn't risk getting hurt, either. Krystal had taught him about the exquisite torture of a marriage gone bad. Night after night, he'd waited for her, wondering who she'd been with, and what he was doing wrong. He kept thinking if he was more...*something*—though he didn't know what—she wouldn't stray. But she had. And he'd been left to pick up the pieces of their broken family.

He knew what he wanted the next time around. He wanted a sure thing. He wasn't going to take any more chances on something as nebulous as love.

## Chapter Five

"I feel like I'm feeding an army," Jill muttered as she grabbed another armful of grocery bags and started through the short hallway that led into the family room.

She'd filled nearly two carts with food and spent more money in an hour than she'd spent on herself in the past four months. She set the bags on the counter and went back for the last couple. While she appreciated that some young man had helped her load the groceries into the car, it would have been a lot more helpful if he could have followed her home and helped her carry them inside.

She slammed the rear door of the utility vehicle, then kicked the door to the garage shut behind her. When she put the last two bags down, she counted.

"...fifteen, sixteen, *seventeen* bags? These boys know how to eat."

Before starting to unload everything, she tossed another load of laundry into the washer. She'd barely gotten the frozen food into the freezer when the phone rang.

She juggled bags of apples in one hand and reached for the receiver with the other.

"Hello, Haynes residence," she said, tucking the phone between her head and shoulder and trying to remember what she'd planned for dinner that night. Did she need to make a salad?

"Jill, it's Kim. Are you still speaking to me?"

Jill set the apples on the counter and bumped the refrigerator door closed. She leaned against the kitchen wall by the phone and sighed. "Kim. I wondered when I'd hear from you."

"Are you mad?"

"Not exactly." She sank onto the sparkling floor. The service she'd hired had sent four cleaning people over. They'd gone through the house like a plague of locusts and had finished in three hours. It would have taken her two, maybe three days.

As she closed her eyes and drew in a breath, she inhaled the scent of pine cleaner and lemon furniture polish.

Her friend sighed. "I'm really sorry. I should have told you the truth, but I knew if I did, you'd say no and then I couldn't go get married and, Jill, I feel so bad."

Amazingly, Kim got that out in one long breath. "Not bad enough," Jill said.

"So you *are* mad."

"No, but I would have liked to have known what I was getting into. Mr. Haynes thought he was hiring a full-time nanny, and I thought I was baby-sitting for a couple of nights."

"But it can't be too awful. You took the job."

"You didn't leave me a lot of choice. The poor man was desperate."

"I'm sorry."

"Don't keep apologizing. I'm not upset." She glanced around at the piles of laundry yet to be folded and the groceries she had to put away. Her gaze strayed to the clock and she realized she had to leave in less than an hour to pick up Danny and C.J. at school.

"This job might be good for me," she said slowly. "At least I don't have to worry about finding a place when you come home from your honeymoon. This job will give me time to think."

"So you don't hate me?"

"No, I don't. How was the wedding?"

"Wonderful. And the honeymoon is even better. Oh, Jill, Brian is everything I dreamed he would be. I can't believe I put off getting married to him for so long. Every day is better than the one before. He's thoughtful and tender. My heart beats faster when he comes into the room. And the sex—"

"Spare me the details," Jill said quickly. "I'll use my imagination."

Kim laughed. "Then you'd better have a good one because—"

"Kim!"

"Okay, I won't tease you anymore." Her friend was silent for a moment. "I do appreciate all you've done. Without you reminding me what was really important, I wouldn't have married Brian."

"You were there for me. When I realized I couldn't stand it anymore, you gave me a place to run to," Jill said. "I owed you. Now we're even."

"How are the boys?"

"Interesting. Very different from Patti and Heather. But I like them."

Over the phone line she heard the sound of a door opening. Kim called her husband over. There was a breath of silence, then a soft giggle.

"Sounds like you two have plans," Jill said. "I'll talk to you when you get back."

"Definitely. We want to have you over for dinner."

"Sounds great. Bye." She hung up the receiver.

Despite the bags of groceries that needed to be emptied, she sat on the floor a little longer. She envied Kim her happiness. Jill tried to remember the last time she'd been excited about a man. She had been married to Aaron for five years, but the thrill wore off very quickly. Had she expected too much, or had she sensed that he was holding back something of himself?

Funny that she never thought about leaving him. Of course, he'd gone out of his way to make her feel obligated to the girls. Maybe that was his way of making sure she was around. Sometimes she felt as if Aaron had played her the way an experienced fisherman plays with a prize bass. Reeling her in slowly, teasing her with just enough line so that the hook sank in deep.

She stood up and put away the rest of the groceries. She glanced at the clock, then made a batch of quick bread. The timer on the oven would turn the heat off at the right time, so it wouldn't overcook. Then she grabbed her purse and keys and headed out to the garage.

Five minutes later she pulled up in front of the school. She joined a long line of cars filled with mothers waiting for their children.

She watched the smiling kids run toward their parents. There hadn't been a lot of laughter in her house when she was growing up. Before the divorce, her parents had fought constantly. After the divorce, they'd spent their time thinking up ways to torment each other. Usually she was the preferred method, each parent playing her against the other. Once she'd grown up and escaped, she'd been willing to do anything to belong to a family, even turn a blind eye to Aaron's real motive for marrying her.

Before she could question her gullibility, she glanced up and saw two boys racing toward the vehicle. They were laughing, and she couldn't help but smile back. She unlocked the car and they tumbled inside. Danny took the front seat. C.J. had had it that morning.

"How was your day?" she asked and waited until they'd put on their seat belts before starting the engine.

"Great," C.J. said. "I've got to do a science project."

"Wonderful," she thought, fighting back a groan. She had a mental picture of a pudding-filled volcano exploding in her freshly cleaned kitchen.

"What about you, Danny?"

Craig's youngest frowned. "I wanna play Pee-Wee ball, but Daddy won't practice with me. He said he would this weekend, but he was gone."

"Your father is working on something special right now. It's important for him to be gone. But he thinks about you and misses you. As soon as he can, he'll start spending more time at home." She paused, wondering if either boy would ask how she knew this bit of information. She didn't, exactly. She was assuming. Because Craig was a decent guy and he genuinely seemed to care about his kids.

"You don't have to practice," C.J. said. "Everyone gets on a team."

"I know." Danny blew his bangs out of his eyes. "But I don't want to be on a *baby* team. I wanna be good."

"Not a problem," Jill said, glancing at him. "We'll help you."

Danny made a face that said he wasn't impressed with the offer.

"I'll have you know that I'm a very good Pee-Wee ball player," she said.

C.J. looked at her and grinned. "You're lying. You've never played Pee-Wee ball."

"Well, I could if I wanted to."

Danny laughed. "You're too big."

"There's a first," she said. "Okay, maybe I haven't played Pee-Wee ball, but I can still help. Your brothers can, too. You'll see, Danny. You'll do great."

"I'll help the kid out," C.J. said. "But Ben won't. He just watches TV or plays video games after school."

Jill didn't like the sound of that. Children needed to get outside and run around. When she'd been a child, she'd often escaped outside to get away from her parents. There, in a tree house, she'd been able to pretend she was somewhere else—in a place where people cared about each other.

She turned the corner and stopped behind the school bus. It turned on its flashing red lights as children began to step down. Ben was one of the last ones off. None of the other children spoke to him as they walked away in groups of twos and threes.

Jill stared at the boy. He had his father's good looks, but he needed to lose weight. His whole body shook when he walked. She frowned, wondering if she was qualified to deal with this problem. Then she realized Ben didn't have anyone else right now. She was going to have to do her best and pray that it was enough.

When he was in the car, she signaled and pulled away from the curb.

"How was your day?" she asked brightly, glancing at him in the rearview mirror.

He looked out the side window and didn't meet her gaze. "Dumb."

"Okay." She thought for a moment, trying to plan the afternoon. It was staying lighter longer so there would be plenty of time. "What's the homework situation for everyone?"

"I don't have any," C.J. said quickly.

"Me, either," Danny piped in.

Ben didn't bother answering.

"No one has homework?" They all shook their heads. "Interesting. No homework on a Monday night. Gee, I'm very surprised. I thought everyone would have *some* homework. But if you say you don't have any, no problem."

They were all lying, she thought, fighting a grin. But she knew how to fix them. She turned on the radio and found one of those stations playing elevator music. The kind with twenty-year-old songs sung by a no-name group. She turned the radio up just loud enough to be annoying, then joined in.

Her natural inclination was to sing off-key and this time she didn't fight it. She sang right along, loudly, making up words if she didn't know them.

The boys stared at each other in disbelief. C.J. clasped his hands around his neck and made a choking sound.

"Jill?" Danny said. "Why are you singing like that?"

"Because I want to. If you don't have homework, then there's plenty of time to listen to my singing. I'm going to take the long way home."

"I've got word lists and a math page," Danny said quickly.

"Really?" she said, sounding surprised.

"I've got Spanish and history," Ben said.

She looked at C.J. in the mirror. He smiled. "Okay, maybe some math and spelling."

She clicked off the radio. "Ah, the truth at last. Okay, here's the plan. We're going to have a snack and do homework for a half hour, then we'll help Danny with his Pee-Wee tryouts. Then, if there's any homework left, it can be done after dinner."

"I don't want to," Ben said.

Jill raised her eyebrows. "Which part doesn't appeal to you?"

"Helping the pip-squeak. I'm gonna watch TV."

"But, Ben, you're the oldest. I would have thought you would want to help your brother out. Don't you play Little League?"

"Not anymore," C.J. said and puffed up his cheeks. "Lard-o is too fat."

Before she could say anything, Ben launched himself at his younger brother. C.J. grabbed him and they started wrestling together. Jill glanced at the street signs. They were only about three blocks from home, but she wanted to prove a point. She pulled to the side of the road and put the car in park.

Danny stared at her. She gave him a wink. In the back seat the boys were grunting and squirming. After a couple of minutes, Ben looked up.

"Aren't you gonna stop us?"

Jill shrugged.

C.J. looked around. "Why'd you pull over here?"

"Because you're acting like animals. It's not safe to drive with loose animals in the car. If you want to settle down, we'll go home. If not, we'll sit here. Oh, look at that girl," she said, pointing to a pretty blonde who was about ten years old. Jill rolled down the window and waved.

"Don't do that," C.J. said from the back of the car. "She'll see you."

"That's the point," Jill said, still smiling and waving. The girl waved back uncertainly.

C.J. groaned and slunk down in his seat. "Please stop."

"Are you two done?" she asked. "If so, then you can apologize, promise not to do it again and we'll leave."

"I'm sorry," C.J. said quickly. "Real sorry. I'll never wrestle with Ben in the car again. I swear!"

She glanced over her shoulder at Ben and raised her eyebrows. "How long do you think it will be until someone you know comes along?"

"I'm sorry, too," he said. "I won't do it again."

"Perfect."

Jill rolled up the window, put the car in drive and headed for home. The last quarter mile was blissfully silent.

After she'd parked in the garage, the boys climbed out. C.J. paused in front of her. "You're not like our other nannies," he said.

"I'm not surprised. Is that a good thing or a bad thing?"

He grinned. "I'll get back to you."

* * *

"I want one more slice," Danny whined, inching closer to the counter.

"Me, too," Ben said, stacking his books on top of each other. The boys had been doing their homework at the kitchen table.

"After we practice and have dinner," Jill said. "You've had your snack already."

Danny eyed the sliced loaf on the counter. "But it was good."

"I'm glad you liked the prune bread. I—"

She stopped talking when she realized all three boys were staring at her. Their eyes widened and their mouths opened.

C.J. recovered first. "*Prune* bread?"

"Yes."

He fell to his knees and started choking. "I'm dying, I'm dying."

Ben followed his lead and dropped to the floor. He writhed in agony. "Prunes. Yuck. She's poisoning us."

Danny stared at his brothers, then her. He wasn't certain who he wanted to side with. Jill ignored his older brothers.

"Don't worry about it," she said. "It was delicious before you knew what it was. It's still delicious. Let's go outside and practice."

She held out her hand. Danny grabbed her fingers. They started for the door. "I know how many slices there were," she called over her shoulder. "So don't even think about sneaking any."

It was warmer today, but still sweatshirt weather. The sky was a brilliant California blue. Tall trees reached for the heavens. The green leaves seemed brighter in the afternoon light, or maybe it was her mood. There was nothing like taking care of three boys to give her something other than herself to think about. Jill wondered if that was part of her problem. She'd had too much free mental time on her hands.

By the time she'd dug out a couple of mitts and a bat, the other two boys had joined them. She didn't comment on Ben's appearance, not wanting to make a big deal of it, but in her heart, she was pleased he wanted to participate.

She tossed them mitts, then found a couple of big plastic balls that wouldn't go far, and wouldn't do any damage if they hit something. Ben came over and took them from her. "I'll pitch," he said.

He'd pulled on a baseball cap. It hid most of his dark hair from view. He wore a loose sweatshirt and jeans. Her heart ached for him. She'd been out of place at home, but at least she'd been able to fit in at school. Ben carried his pain with him everywhere.

She gave him a quick smile and gently touched his cheek. He stiffened at the contact but didn't pull away. His dark gaze met hers. Some emotion flickered there. She couldn't read it, but she knew it was hurting him. She wanted to pull him close and hug him until he felt better, but she didn't have the right. Even if she did, Ben wouldn't let her. He was as prickly as a porcupine.

"Batter up," he called, moving to the center of the yard.

There was more room in the front than in the back, so that was where they played. Jill stayed in the background, filling in where she was needed. C.J. was fast and talented, with the grace of a natural athlete. Ben had the same raw ability, but his weight slowed him down. He could pitch with perfect precision, but he got winded if he tried to run the bases. Even six-year-old Danny could catch him.

Jill stared at the youngest of Craig Haynes's boys. Danny stood hunched over his bat, his face scrunched up in concentration. Ben released the ball. Danny swung and missed.

"Keep your eyes open," C.J. called from the out-field.

"I am."

"Then hit the dumb ball."

"I'm tryin'." Frustration filled Danny's voice, but he didn't give up. He tossed the ball back to Ben and hunched over again.

"Is he standing right?" she asked, coming up to stand behind him. "Maybe it's his shoulders."

Danny looked at her and grimaced. "It's not my shoulders. Ben and C.J. are better than me."

"They're also older and have had more practice. You're going to make it. You're determined, and sometimes that's more important than raw talent."

He beamed, then hunched over. Jill moved back and studied him. He didn't have his brothers' dark hair or eyes. He must take after his mother. Despite having checked on the cleaning crew while they worked and going into all the bedrooms to put clean laundry on the beds, she hadn't seen a picture of the boys' mother. While she was curious about Krystal Haynes, she wasn't comfortable with snooping.

Ben pitched again.

"Keep your eyes open," Jill called.

Danny swung hard. The bat cracked against the plastic ball and sent it sailing toward the heavens.

"You did it!" she said and clapped her hands. Danny tossed off his hat in celebration.

Ben jumped to snag the ball, but he missed.

"Jeez, fatty, can't you do anything?" C.J. said as he raced toward it. He caught the ball in his glove, went down on one knee, rolled onto his back and came up, still holding the ball in his glove. "Craig Haynes, Jr., wins the national championship." He bowed to an imaginary crowd.

Ben threw off his glove and started for the house.

"Ben," she called.

The boy kept walking. He stalked through the garage. She ran after him. "Ben, wait. I know C.J. is being a pain, but you're doing great. Please don't leave."

In the background, she heard a car pull up at the curb.

Ben turned to look at her. Tears swam in his eyes, but he blinked them back. "Go back where you came from. We don't need you here. We don't like you." With that, he opened the door to the family room and stepped into the house. The door slammed shut behind him.

"Daddy, Daddy!"

She turned and saw C.J. and Danny running toward their father. She hadn't seen Craig since Saturday night. He was gone when she woke up Sunday morning and didn't come home until after she went to bed.

He wore his uniform, but he'd left his hat inside his car. The sunlight caught the dark wavy hair. He was tall and broad, and for some reason, her heart began fluttering foolishly in her chest. She told herself it was just the uniform, or the strangeness of the situation. Maybe it was a bit of indigestion. Maybe she'd eaten her slice of prune bread too quickly.

The two boys embraced their father. He squatted down and hugged them. She liked the way he touched them so easily. Some fathers had trouble showing affection. A hug went a long way toward making many problems right. After all, Craig had made her feel better, just by holding her in his arms.

She didn't want to remember that. Nor did she want to remember how good she'd felt sitting on his lap. It hadn't seemed to matter that they were practically strangers. It wasn't like her to expose her emotions like that. She wasn't sure what had happened. Better that it be the late hour of the night and not the man. She knew the danger of getting involved.

"How's everything going?" Craig asked as she approached.

"It was going fine until a couple of minutes ago. We're helping Danny so he'll make a good Pee-Wee team."

"I don't want to be with the babies," his youngest said loudly.

"You won't be," Craig said. He glanced around. "Where's Ben?"

"He went inside," Danny said. "He got mad when he couldn't catch a ball."

"That's not exactly what happened," Jill reminded him.

C.J. stepped away from his father and shuffled his feet. "He *is* fat."

Jill dropped to her knees and took C.J.'s hands in hers. He had his father's eyes and hair, too. Both the older boys definitely took after their dad.

She stared at the boy. "Ben knows he's overweight. I think it bothers him. What do you think?"

C.J. shrugged uncomfortably. "Why does he have to be like that? It's gross."

"Don't you think he wants to change? But it's hard. When you make fun of him, he feels bad. When he feels bad, he eats. I'm not saying this is your fault, because it isn't. But you're not helping."

C.J. drew in a deep breath. "I'm sorry."

"Maybe you should apologize to your brother instead of me."

"Jeez, do I have to?"

She smiled. "Yeah, you do."

"Bummer." He gave her a quick grin and started for the house.

Jill sank onto the grass and buried her face in her hands. "Maybe we should have kept that one-week trial," she said. "After all this, you're going to be the one wanting me to leave."

"Don't go, Jill," Danny said and flung himself at her.

She caught the young boy and pulled him onto her lap. His sturdy arms wrapped around her back and he hugged her close.

"Don't go," he repeated. "I like having you here."

She brushed his light brown hair from his eyes and smiled. "I'm glad someone likes me."

She held him tight. It had been a long time since she'd hugged a child. After the divorce, she'd been cut off from the girls. A cruel and unusual punishment, but there hadn't been anyone to take her side. Her heart filled with an achy kind of joy and she wondered if this was going to cost her later.

She released Danny. "Up with you, young man. We've got work to do."

Danny slid onto the grass, then sprang to his feet. Craig held out his hand to her. She took it reluctantly. As she'd expected, the second their fingers touched, hot, fluttery sensations raced down her arm to settle in her breasts and between her thighs. She allowed him to pull her to her feet, hoping madly that it really was indigestion and not something more deadly, like attraction.

When she was on her feet, Craig didn't release her hand. He glanced at her fingers, then returned his gaze to her face. "Thanks for what you said about Ben. I don't know what to do about him."

"Have you talked to anyone?"

"A counselor, you mean?"

She nodded.

"No, but maybe I should. I don't want him to be so unhappy, and I worry about his health. He's just a kid. This should be a fun time for him. But it isn't."

The father shared the son's pain, but this hurt couldn't be hugged away. "I wish I had the answers," she said. "I've got a few ideas. Maybe we can talk about them later."

"I'd like that."

He released her hand and bent over to pick up Danny. The boy looped his arms around his father's neck. Craig placed his hand at the small of her back and urged her toward the house. She fought against the heat spiraling through her middle. She didn't like that this house of males was getting to her.

"Are you in for the evening?" she asked, hoping he would be leaving soon so she could get her heart rate back to normal.

"I've got a late meeting, but I'll be here until nine. I thought I could help with dinner."

"I will, too," Danny said, giving her his best smile.

"Great." So much for regaining her equilibrium.

"Jill made prune bread," the boy told his father.

"Good."

"You like it?"

"Of course. Anything homemade is a treat."

"Oh. Okay. I like it, too."

Jill glanced at them. The ache in her chest intensified. Craig Haynes had everything she'd ever wanted. With every word he spoke, with every action, he and his sons invited her into their lives. Staying disconnected—*not* getting involved—was going to be harder than she'd thought.

## Chapter Six

Craig shut Danny's door. C.J.'s light was already out. That left only Ben. He hesitated outside his oldest's room. Ben had been unusually quiet during dinner. Not belligerent, just thoughtful. Was he thinking about how unhappy he was? Was he wishing his father hadn't let him down?

Craig remembered all the times *his* father had let him down. In the end, he'd hated his old man. Would Ben grow up to feel the same way? Craig didn't want to think about that. He didn't want to know that he'd failed his son so badly. He wanted to believe it wasn't too late, but he didn't know what to do to bridge the chasm already between them.

He crossed the hallway and tapped on Ben's door. At the muffled "Come in," he entered.

He glanced around, surprised. All the boys had cleaned their rooms. When the service had come through that morning, everything had been dusted and vacuumed. It made a big difference. He should have done it months ago.

Ben sat up in bed playing a hand-held video game. He didn't bother glancing up as his father entered. Craig settled on the chair by the desk and waited.

For a few minutes there was only the faint sound of a battle being fought on the tiny screen. Then there was an explosion. Ben grimaced and looked up. "Yeah, Dad?"

"I just came to say good-night."

Ben looked away, as if to say he knew there had to be more. There was.

"How was your day at school?"

"Fine."

"Classes going okay?"

"I guess."

The boy stared at his video game but didn't turn it on. Craig couldn't believe he felt this awkward. This was his kid. They should at least be friends. He grimaced. At one time they had been. But things had changed. Ben had been hit the hardest by the divorce, and later by Krystal's death. He had been old enough to really remember his mother.

He cleared his throat. "Jill seems to be working out."

"I guess."

One "fine" and two "I guesses." They sure were bonding now. "I really appreciate you taking the time to help Danny today. He wants to do well for Pee-Wee tryouts."

"They don't turn anyone away."

"I know, but if he's halfway decent, he'll get on a better team. Anyway, thanks for doing that."

Ben didn't answer. Craig wondered if the boy felt as uncomfortable as he did. But, damn it, he was the adult. He had to try.

He leaned forward and rested his elbows on his knees, then laced his fingers together. There was a time when he and Ben had had plenty to say to each other. Years ago they'd been buddies. C.J. and Danny had been babies, but Ben had been his friend. He hated to see that change.

"You going out for Little League?" he asked, hoping to spark some interest.

Something close to pain flashed across Ben's face. "It's dumb," he said, and turned toward the wall. He put the video game on the nightstand, then settled down on the mattress. Craig knew he'd been dismissed.

He rose to his feet and crossed to the bed. He bent over and touched his son's arm. "I love you, Ben. If you want to talk or anything..." His voice trailed off. "I'll always make time for you, son." His throat tightened and he walked out of the room.

He paused at the top of the stairs. He was doing a poor job as a father, and he had no one to blame but himself. When had he stopped being a friend as well as a parent? When had he first been afraid that they would want more than he had to give?

He couldn't point his finger to a particular day, or hour, but he knew it involved Krystal. She'd rattled his confidence and changed the shape of his world. He'd been stripped of his pride and left bleeding. The boys were the true casualties of that particular war.

He had to stop avoiding his kids, he told himself. It wasn't making anything better. It only accentuated the problem. As soon as this assignment was over he would—

The phone rang. He thought about getting it but knew Jill would pick it up. It was probably just the station asking him to come in earlier.

As he started down the stairs, he realized he didn't have to wait for the assignment to be over before making changes. He could start now with small things. He didn't want his kids becoming strangers.

When he walked into the kitchen, Jill was just hanging up the receiver. She scribbled something on a small pad of paper.

"Was that the station?" he asked.

She glanced up. Color stained her cheeks. "Um, not exactly." She looked at the floor, then at the note and the refrigerator, before settling her gaze on the center of his chest.

"Someone named Austin just called. He said to tell you that it's been so long since he's seen you that he's forgotten what you and the boys look like. Call him and set up a date for a barbecue or suffer the consequences."

Jill's blush deepened. Craig leaned against the doorframe and folded his arms over his chest. He fought back a smile. "What else did he say?"

"Well, he said that—" She cleared her throat. "He said if I'm the reason you've been laying low, then it's about time and I'm welcome too."

He had the fleeting thought that life would be pretty damn pleasant if Jill *was* the reason he hadn't spent time with his family. "What did you tell him?"

"That I'm just the new nanny. I tried to convince him I was old and matronly, but he won't believe me. Who is that guy?"

"A friend of the family, but we all think of him as a Haynes. Austin's got a research company. He does work with heat-resistant polymers and other substances. Very high-tech stuff. It's used in the space shuttle and for certain manufacturing processes."

"He didn't sound like a scientist."

"He doesn't look like one either," he said, remembering how all the women in Glenwood had sighed over his friend's good looks. He figured it was the earring that got to the women. Glenwood wasn't an earring sort of town.

She motioned to the full coffeepot on the counter. "I thought you might like some before you went back to the station."

"Sure. Thanks."

He walked to the table and pulled out one of the chairs. After turning it neatly, he sat, straddling it and resting his forearms on the back. She poured coffee into a mug and brought it over black.

He smiled his thanks. "Travis and Austin became friends first. Then he was just part of the family." He frowned, trying to remember all that had happened. "He was gone for a while. He stole a car and was sent to a juvenile facility. It ended up being the best thing for him. He met a man who taught him about chemistry and manufacturing. The old guy got him a scholarship, and Austin never looked back. His company has grown. It's privately owned." He grinned. "Just the five of us."

Jill took the seat opposite. "Five of you?"

"Austin, of course, and me and my three brothers."

She shook her head. "I'm confused. You guys are all partners?"

"Yes." He took a sip of coffee.

She brushed her bangs off her forehead and frowned. "If the company is doing well, why aren't you rich?"

"I can afford a full-time nanny, can't I?"

"How much is the company worth?"

He shrugged. "Millions."

"And you work as a cop?"

"I want to."

"But you don't have to?"

He thought about the last financial statement. "No, I don't have to." None of his brothers did. But money wasn't important. It never had been. They hadn't grown up lacking things; they'd grown up lacking love.

"You are too weird," Jill said, pushing to her feet. "You want some prune bread?"

"Sure. And why am I weird? Lots of people enjoy their work."

"I guess. Although when I was at the insurance company, if someone had offered me a large income, I think I would have quit that very day."

"You have to do something with your time. All of us work."

"Your brothers?" She sliced the rest of the loaf onto a plate and set it in front of him. Then she got a diet soda from the refrigerator and returned to her seat. "Maybe it's a faulty gene pool," she said. "You all have an unnatural desire to be employed."

"You could be right." He snagged a slice and took a bite. "I've thought about quitting, but I couldn't figure out what I'd do with myself. Besides, I like making a difference. Like on this case. If we can nail the bastards preying on the elderly, then a whole bunch of people will be saved a lot of heartache."

Her full lips curved up at the corners. "An honest-to-God hero. I thought you guys only existed in the movies."

Her praise made him uncomfortable. "I'm no hero. Just look at my kids."

"You mean Ben, don't you?"

He nodded and pushed away the plate. "I don't know where I went wrong with him. I guess I've been working too much. I don't know him anymore. We don't have anything to talk about."

"He's unhappy about his weight," Jill said.

"I know. Maybe I should hook him up with a counselor. Or one of those camps over the summer. But I hate to separate the boys. What do you think?"

"I understand your concerns. Has he been on a diet before?"

"No. We talked about it, but Mrs. Miller never thought there was a problem. She said he would outgrow it. But then she was a large woman herself. Since she left, no one has been around long enough to do anything."

"He needs to lose the weight, but if he's never been on a diet, then maybe we could try that before sending him away to a camp."

Craig liked the sound of the word "we" on her lips. It made him feel that he wasn't in this alone.

She waved her diet soda in the air. "After the divorce, I gained about fifteen pounds. It doesn't sound like much, but at five-one and three-quarters—"

He laughed. "Can't you just say five-two?"

She straightened in her chair. "Number one, we aren't all blessed by being tall, and number two, I'm not going to exaggerate. Five-one and three-quarters is a very nice height."

He was willing to admit it looked pretty fine on her. He held up his hands in a gesture of surrender. "You're right. Sorry for interrupting."

She sniffed, then continued. "On me, fifteen pounds is about two dress sizes. I had the body tone of a water balloon. Anyway, I took it off with a low-fat diet and exercise. Now I'm a walking fiend. Maybe we could try the same with Ben. I think the key is to not let him get hungry or feel deprived. I know kids need a certain amount of fat for growth and energy. Let me talk to Ben and do some research in the library. Maybe we can work out a program he can live with."

"Thanks," he said, knowing he owed her a lot more. "You didn't sign up for this when you agreed to look after my kids."

"Maybe not, but I'm having a good time. It's nice to think about someone other than myself."

He glanced at his watch. "I've got to go. Bingo gets out soon and I want to be there. Several of the accidents have occurred at this time of night and on the same street."

He rose to his feet and Jill did the same. She circled around the table and placed her hand on his forearm. The top of her head barely came to his shoulder, but her spine was pure steel, and her touch, while gentle, offered strength.

"You're doing a good thing," she said.

"At the expense of what? My kids?"

"They understand, and they're proud of you."

"It's not enough."

She gave him a half smile. "Maybe not, but it's a start."

Their gazes locked. The pure green of her irises reminded him of cat eyes. Her expression was just as

enigmatic. He didn't know what she was thinking.
With any luck, she couldn't read his mind, either. Because he wasn't busy being grateful for her advice, or
planning low-fat meals for his kid. Instead he was
wondering what her mouth would taste like against his
and how she would feel in his arms. The memory of
holding her on his lap was enough to fuel his already-
active imagination. He wanted to bury himself inside
her, touching her, kissing her until she was wild with
passion, then drained by fulfillment.

His arousal made itself known against the fly of his
uniform trousers. He ignored the throbbing.

"Thanks for talking with me tonight," he said.
"And thanks for the advice." It had been a long time
since he'd been able to talk with anyone.

"My pleasure." An emotion flickered in her cat eyes.
He almost convinced himself she wanted him to kiss
her, but he knew it was just wishful thinking.

He walked out of the room and toward the garage.
He was a damn fool if he started projecting his desires
onto Jill. She'd made it clear this was nothing but a
temporary job for her, and he knew better than to get
involved in something that wasn't a sure thing.

It was barely six when Jill knocked on Ben's door.
She was a little nervous, not sure what her reception
would be. Would he be mad that she was trying to
help?

She opened the door and stepped into the dark
room. The sun was just up and little light shone
through the space between the shade and the edge of
the window.

As her eyes adjusted to the darkness she could make
out Ben sleeping on his side, facing the door. Lying

down, tucked under the covers, he didn't seem as grown-up. There was a sweetness about him that made her heart ache with longing for a child of her own.

She sat on the edge of the mattress and shook his arm. "Ben, it's Jill."

"Huh?" He raised his head and blinked, then stared at the clock. A scowl pulled his eyebrows together. "It's an hour early. It's only six. Can't you tell time?"

So much for the warm welcome. "I'm going for a walk. I thought you might want to come with me."

He rolled away from her. "You thought wrong. I don't want to take a walk."

"I like to walk in the morning. It's good exercise and helps keep my weight down. But the best part is no one has to know. I'll be back before C.J. and Danny wake up."

She waited, counting her heartbeats. At ten, Ben turned toward her. Distrust and hope warred in his eyes. "Yeah?"

"Yeah." She stood up. "I'll wait for you downstairs. Put on something comfortable and athletic shoes."

Five minutes later, he met her by the front door. When they walked outside, she inhaled the sweet smell of morning. It was still early enough to need a jacket, even with the walking, but it was going to be another warm, perfect California spring day.

They walked in silence to the end of the block. Ben seemed to keep up with her easily, so she increased her pace. After another few minutes of quiet, she pointed out a budding flower. He didn't say anything. She tried to console herself with the fact that if he didn't talk, he couldn't be sarcastic.

A neighbor's dog trotted out to greet them. She paused long enough to pat it. Ben scratched its ears, too, and when she glanced at him, she caught a faint smile. Maybe, she thought, casually crossing her fingers for luck. Just maybe this was going to work.

When they'd been walking for nearly twenty minutes, she said, "I think I'd like to make your lunch for a while. Can you bring food from home or would all your friends laugh at you?"

He shrugged. "About half the kids bring their lunches. It's not so bad. But in a bag, okay? The real nerds still use lunch boxes."

"No lunch boxes, I swear." She smiled. "I'll give you lots of food. You won't be hungry. You can eat it all or just eat some of it. If you don't like something I make, then tell me and I'll change it. All I ask in return is that you don't trade it for junk food. Do you drink milk at school?"

"Nah. It's not cold enough. There's a soda machine, or I get juice."

"Both of those are fine." She knew she was treading on delicate ground here. She didn't know Ben very well and he didn't trust her yet. If she said the wrong thing, he might never respond to her. "It's not about how much you eat, but what you eat. There's lots of fun things to have. Cookies, frozen yogurt. It won't be hard."

He didn't say anything. They turned around and started for the house.

"I want to help you, Ben," she said, not looking at him. "If you want me to. No one would have to know. It could be our secret."

Silence. Jill drew in a deep breath. She'd tried. The rest was up to him.

When they reached their house, she stopped by the porch and stretched out her legs. Ben watched her for a moment, then did the same. He finished before her and pushed open the front door, then paused.

"Can you make my lunch today?" he asked, staring at his shoes.

Happiness filled her and she had to fight back a smile. "Sure. I'd be happy to."

"Thanks, Jill." He raced inside.

Jill turned her head toward the faint breeze rustling the leaves on the trees and told herself the burning in her eyes was just from the dryness of the wind.

"Come on, batter, batter, batter," Jill called and clapped her hands together. "Hit it clean over the house."

Danny glanced over his shoulder at her. "Ji-ill, it's just a plastic ball. It's not gonna go that far."

"How do you know until you try?"

He grinned, then hunched over the imaginary plate. Ben pitched perfectly. The ball came sailing straight and true. Danny struck with all his might, dropped the bat and started running.

Jill leaned back against the tree and watched the three boys at play. It had been a week since she'd arrived at the Haynes household. In some ways, it felt as if she'd always been here. They'd settled into a routine, and she was getting to know the boys.

She and Ben had walked together for the past four mornings. Slowly, he was opening up to her, telling her about school and his few friends. He was self-conscious about his appearance, but when he forgot about it, he was funny and bright and a pleasure to be with. So far, he'd taken the lunches she made and given her enough feedback on the food to convince her he was actually eating it. She'd made a few low-fat changes in the evening meals, so he didn't have to have a different menu. He followed her lead, taking more of what she took more of, less of the dishes she ignored.

She turned her attention to the youngest of the Haynes boys. Danny was a sweetheart. He gave everything a hundred percent and wore his heart on his sleeve. He would never be the athlete his brothers were, but it wasn't for lack of trying. Even as C.J. caught the ball and started toward their makeshift third base, Danny kept on running. It didn't matter that his brother was bigger or faster. Danny was the little engine that could. One day that trait would help make him successful.

Then there was C.J. Jill studied the middle of the three boys. Craig Junior had his father's good looks and smooth delivery. He had that innate ability to say the right thing at the right time. He had enough charm to be a gigolo in his next life, although she hoped he chose something more stable for this one.

All in all, she was pretty happy with how her job was going. It wasn't tough duty and she was well paid.

"It's C.J.'s turn to hit," Ben said.

"But I wanna try again," Danny whined.

"You got tagged out. It's not your turn."

"Yes, it is!" Danny stamped his foot.

"If you're gonna act like a baby, you can't play," Ben said.

C.J. strolled over to join his brothers, but he didn't take sides.

"I'm not a baby."

"Are too."

Danny dropped his bat and curled his hands into fists. "Am not. And you're just a fat old mobyhead."

C.J. started to laugh. Jill straightened up. Mobyhead?

"Boys," she started, but it was too late. Ben tore off his glove and dropped it on the ground.

"This is stupid," he said, and headed for the house.

"You come back here," Danny said. "You help me. Ben, you have to help me."

His big brother ignored him and kept on going.

Danny ran to Jill. Tears streamed down his cheeks. "He has to help me. I want to do better."

"Maybe you should have thought about that before you called him names."

"He called me names, too."

Danny had a point. "Okay, that was wrong. However, did you do anything to make him think you were acting like a baby?"

C.J. strolled over. "I don't mind missing my turn."

Danny sniffed. "I didn't mean to," he said softly. The sun caught his light brown hair and turned it the color of gold.

"I'm not the one you have to apologize to. And while we're on the subject, what's a mobyhead?"

Danny flushed, but C.J. laughed. "Danny doesn't want to say a bad word. You know."

She shook her head. She didn't know.

"Moby. Like that whale book."

*"Moby Dick?"* She frowned, then said, "Oh, I get it." She glared at Danny. "You were calling your brother a dickhead? Danny, I'm ashamed of you."

He dropped his chin to his chest and sniffed. "Sorry."

"You already said that. Once again, I'm not the person you need to apologize to. But before you go in, I want to remind you, we do not use that kind of language."

"But he called me a baby."

"He's worked with you every single afternoon this week. He's pitched to you and has given you advice on how to get better. Did you ever thank him? Did you ever tell him you appreciated his efforts? No, you got mad and called him names."

By now Danny's tears were flowing fast and furious. He glared at her. "I hate you," he said and ran inside.

Jill sighed. So much for things going well. C.J. picked up the mitts, the bat and the ball. She glanced at him. "I believe it's now your turn to be mad at me."

"Nah. You're okay. For a girl."

They looked at each other and smiled. She rose to her feet and ruffled his hair. "You're not so bad yourself."

As they walked to the house, C.J. took hold of her hand. She was surprised, but didn't pull back. In that moment she realized she hadn't expected him to be the first one to steal her heart. But a piece had just been magically removed. How much more damage would this family do, before she had the chance to get away?

## *Chapter Seven*

Everyone slept in on Saturday. Jill got up around seven, showered and put on jeans and a sweatshirt. She had to admit that this job was really easy to dress for. She sure didn't miss having to put on a suit and panty hose every day.

She made a detour on her way to the kitchen and peeked out the window. Craig's car was parked in front of the house. It was strange to never know if he was home or not. Worse, once she realized he was in the house—sleeping upstairs—her stomach gave a little flutter. She wondered what he slept in.... She pressed her palm to her belly and willed herself to stay calm. It didn't matter if he was home. It didn't matter if he wasn't. She wasn't interested. He was her employer, nothing else. She wasn't going to get involved.

And pigs landed regularly at the airport just outside town.

She turned around and headed for the kitchen, trying to justify her attraction to Craig. He was a handsome man. She hadn't been with a man in a couple of years. The last few months of her marriage had been during the custody trial for the girls and she and Aaron hadn't been intimate much. She hadn't dated at all since then, so she was simply reacting to the proximity of an available male. It would have been the same with anyone. This wasn't specifically about Craig.

As she collected the ingredients to make pancakes, she thought it was pretty stupid to lie to herself. After all, she knew the truth. She might not like it, but she knew it.

In the two weeks she'd been a member of the Haynes household, she'd had several late-night or early-morning talks with her employer. If he wasn't home for dinner, she left something out for him. Usually she heard him in the kitchen and came out to see how he was. At first she'd been a little self-conscious, but then she reminded herself that he'd already seen her in a skimpy robe that first day he showed up at Kim's house. So seeing her in a terry-cloth one that brushed the floor was hardly exciting.

In the silent hours of night, he talked about his work, and she brought him up-to-date on the children. They talked about who was angry with whom, who was doing homework and who had broken what. In the time since her divorce, she'd forgotten how volatile childish tempers could be. One minute there were screams of hatred and the next they were playing together. She figured as long as everyone got along in the end, she didn't mind.

She hadn't heard Craig come in the previous night. Idly, she wondered if he was home for the weekend. He hadn't had a day off since she arrived two weeks ago. The boys told her that he usually worked regular hours, but this special assignment demanded more. They weren't sure what he was doing, but they knew it was something they could be proud of.

They worried about their dad, and he worried about them. She poured milk into the pancake batter and stirred it vigorously. Aaron had always been concerned with how things looked, while Craig worried about how things really were. Too bad she hadn't seen her ex was a jerk before she married him.

When the batter was finished, she rinsed off the first strawberries of the season, cut them up and put them in a bowl. Then she started coffee. When the pot was dripping steadily, she went upstairs to wake the boys.

C.J. was already sitting up and reading. He gave her a smile and said he would be right down.

Danny stirred sleepily. "What's for breakfast, Jill?" he asked.

She bent over and brushed his hair from his eyes. "Pancakes."

He smiled. "Good. I love pancakes. I can eat a hundred."

She bent over and kissed his cheek. "Then that's how many I'm going to make for you."

She stood up and moved into Ben's room. When she opened the door, he opened his eyes and glanced at her, then at the clock.

"It's late."

"I know. Breakfast is ready."

Dark eyes met hers. "What about our walk?"

"Everyone gets to take a day off. Instead of walking, you can play outside with your brothers today. I don't know if your dad is going to stay home or not, but maybe we can do something as a group. The zoo, or a park. Don't worry, I'll make sure you get exercise.''

He didn't return her smile. Instead, his big dark eyes widened. He flushed slightly. "Thanks, Jill."

"You're welcome." Her throat was uncomfortably tight as she backed out of the room.

She paused by Craig's room but didn't knock. She wasn't sure what time he'd come home, and he probably needed his sleep. He'd been working impossible hours since she arrived and for who knew how long before that.

Involuntarily, she brushed her fingers against the smooth surface of the door. Images sprang into her mind. Images of what Craig might look like on the other side of this door. She didn't want to think about it, but she couldn't help herself. Was he lying there in a tangle of sheets, his long, lean, athletic body bare? She knew he was alone. Craig wasn't the type to bring a woman home. She wondered what he did for sex. Was there a discreet lady friend somewhere? Did he have a type, and if he did, what was it?

"None of my business," she said softly, and turned toward the stairs.

Ten minutes later she slipped the first four pancakes off the electric griddle and put them on a warming plate. Ten minutes after that, all three boys sat around the table drinking juice and laughing. Jill served them. Ben stared at the pancakes uncertainly.

She leaned over his shoulder and set down the bowl of berries. "Have all the fruit and syrup you want," she said quietly. "Stay away from the butter."

He gave her a grateful smile.

"What are we going to do today?" Danny asked. "I finished my homework yesterday."

"Me, too," C.J. said, then stuck a piece of pancake in his mouth. "Is Dad home?" he mumbled.

"Yes," she said. "Don't talk with your mouth full."

"Yes'm." He barely moved his lips as he spoke the word. She had to turn away to hide a grin.

"Do you think Daddy will stay with us today?" Danny asked.

"Nah, he's gonna be too busy," Ben answered for her.

Jill didn't like his answer, but she didn't have a better one. Craig hadn't told her his plans. Maybe she should tell him that his sons assumed he wouldn't have time for them.

She got up to pour herself more coffee. There was a creak on the stairs. She set the pot down, turned and was instantly pleased she wasn't holding anything as fragile as a glass coffeepot.

Craig walked into the kitchen. There was nothing extraordinary about the action. She'd seen him walk into the kitchen before. But she'd never seen him out of uniform, and, frankly, he took her breath away.

He was dressed simply. Bare feet, worn jeans, a sweatshirt. Thousands, maybe millions of men wore the same casual clothes on the weekend. But other men weren't Craig.

His dark hair was still damp from the shower and smoothed away from his face. One stubborn lock brushed against his forehead. His jaw was clean-shaven, his smile easy. The university logo on the sweatshirt had seen several dozen washings. The once dark blue fabric had faded. But it looked soft, and it highlighted the width of his shoulders. His jeans hung loosely on his legs, the denim lighter at the seams, knees and, intriguingly, at the crotch.

Nothing about his clothing was overtly erotic, yet she couldn't stop the ripple of need that coursed through her. Her heart pounded hard and loud in her chest and her palms were suddenly sweaty.

Their eyes met. She sent up a quick prayer that he couldn't read what she'd been thinking. It would be too humiliating.

"Morning," he said.

The three boys turned as one. "Dad!" They tumbled from their seats and into his arms. In the confusion of hugs and questions, Jill tried to draw in a steadying breath.

"How many pancakes would you like?" she asked, and was pleased when her voice sounded normal.

"A plateful. I'm starved. I didn't get dinner." He glanced at the table, then at her. "This looks great. Thanks, Jill."

He'd said her name a hundred times before, but this time was different. This time the sound skittered across her skin, making the hairs on the back of her neck stand up.

"My pleasure." She poured more batter on the griddle.

"Are you going to work today?" Danny asked as he stepped back and stared at his father.

Craig leaned over and ruffled his hair. "Nope. I'm off for the whole weekend."

"Wow! Can we practice baseball?"

"Sure. Whatever you want."

The three boys grabbed him again and held on tight. Craig turned away from the table, dragging them along. C.J. laughed. Even Ben giggled.

"You boys going to let me go?" Craig asked.

"No!" they answered as one.

With that, Craig dropped to his knees, taking the boys with him. They swarmed over him, like bees on a flower. They were one mass of tickling, wrestling, hugging bodies.

"I've got you now."

"I'll get you back."

"Let's tickle Dad."

"Let's not."

Bits of conversation overlapped. Jill turned the pancakes and stared at the Haynes males enjoying themselves. She felt as if she were on the outside of the inner circle. The familiarity of the emotion startled her. In that moment, she realized she'd spent much of her marriage on the outside looking in. She'd fooled herself into believing that she belonged, but it wasn't true. It had never been true.

She set the cooked pancakes on the warming tray.

"You boys planning to finish your breakfast anytime soon?" she asked.

"No!" Danny said. He was tugging on his father's leg. Ben had wrestled one of Craig's arms to the ground and was trying to pin it there. C.J. lunged for her.

She tried to jump back, but she wasn't fast enough. He tugged on her leg. Her knee gave, and she started to fall. She didn't know what to brace herself on. She didn't want to hurt any of the boys.

Before she could figure out what to do, Craig twisted free and grabbed her. He spun her as she fell, so she landed across his lap. Her bottom connected with his rock-hard thighs.

She barely had time to absorb the feeling of his body so close to hers when Danny flung himself on top of them both. His bony legs splayed over her hips and he leaned down to press his nose against hers.

"I'm the winner," he said.

She smiled. "You are?"

"Yep."

Craig laughed. She felt the vibration of sound against her arm, which was pinned against his chest. C.J. came up behind her and started tickling her. She shrieked.

"Stop that," she demanded between gasps.

"She's real ticklish," C.J. crowed in delight.

Ben started to attack, too.

Jill tried to slip away, but she was trapped. Craig leaned over, trying to shield her with his body. As his weight shifted, they all tumbled together, a wild assortment of arms and tangled legs.

She laughed until her sides ached and she couldn't catch her breath. For that moment, she was a part of the family. She knew it was temporary, but she didn't care. The warmth and happiness thawed the ice around her soul.

"Okay, boys, get up," Craig said. "While we finish breakfast, we'll decide what we're going to do this weekend. But whatever it is, we're going to do it together."

"Everything?" Danny asked as he stood up. "Even go to the bathroom?"

"You are so weird," Ben said and lunged for his brother. Danny shrieked and took off around the table. In a matter of seconds, all three of them were racing around the room.

Craig shook his head. "I think my brothers and I were worse. I don't know how my mother stood it."

"I'm sure she loved you all."

Jill stood up and brushed off her behind. Without thinking, she offered her hand to Craig. He took it and rose to his feet. Once there, he towered over her. Six feet of sexually enticing male.

"What do *you* want to do this weekend?" Craig asked her.

"I get a vote?"

"Sure, you're part of the family."

C.J. stopped running and leaned against her. "Let's go bike riding."

Danny flopped into his seat. His light brown hair fell into his eyes. "I wanna play baseball."

"I want to go to the movies," Ben said.

All four males stared at her. Jill was torn between wanting to belong and reminding them that she was just the temporary help. She would only be here for another three weeks. Not that she'd seen Craig interviewing anyone else for her job.

If she were smart, she would ask for the day off. Craig was home; he could handle the kids by himself. She opened her mouth to say just that.

"I'd like to not have to cook dinner tonight," she said, then wondered where that had come from.

"Done," Craig said, pulling out the chair at the head of the table. "Everyone gets his or her wish."

There was a collective cheer.

Jill walked to the counter and put four pancakes on a plate. If she'd known Craig was going to be granting wishes so easily, she might have asked for something more intriguing.

They stopped to rest in the park. Craig sat on the ground with his back against a tree, while Danny flopped next to him. Ben, C.J. and Jill sprawled across a picnic table, using the attached bench seats as foot-rests.

Overhead the sun was bright, and the temperature was just warm enough not to be cool. As his boys chattered, Craig tried to remember the last time he'd taken the day off and done nothing except have fun. Usually there were errands to run and the boys had activities. But today everyone seemed to be content to be together.

"We can take the short way home," he said, then stretched. "Of course the long way goes right by the ice-cream shop."

C.J. grinned down at him. "Gee, Dad, let's go the long way."

Jill leaned over and bumped C.J.'s shoulder. "And people say you're not too smart."

He laughed. "I'm very smart."

"So smart you've got Krissie Nelson doing your math homework for you. Don't think I haven't caught on."

C.J.'s eyes widened and he looked as startled as a mouse facing down a tiger. "How'd you know that?" he asked, then clamped his hand over his mouth.

Ben laughed. "You blew it, bozo. Now you're dead meat."

C.J. looked at Jill. "She just did it at recess a couple times. How'd you find out?"

Jill arched her eyebrows. "I know everything." She touched his face. "You left your homework out on the kitchen table yesterday morning and Krissie had written a note on the paper. Cheating is stupid and you're not. Okay?"

C.J. flushed. "Yeah. Sorry." He glanced at his father. "Dad?"

Craig was torn between wanting to ground C.J. for the next fifteen years and being impressed with how Jill had handled the situation. He fought down the flicker of annoyance that she hadn't discussed it with him, then realized that in the past four days he'd only been home to sleep for a couple of hours.

"I expect better of you," he said quietly.

C.J. sucked in a breath as if he'd been mortally wounded. "Dad—" He broke off and stared at the trees for a moment. "I won't do it again."

Jill stood up and jumped to the ground. "Let's go get some ice cream," she said and headed for her bike. Everyone followed.

When C.J. walked by, Craig snagged his arm. Father and son looked at each other for a moment, then C.J. mumbled, "I'm sorry," and ducked into his embrace. Craig held him tightly for a moment.

"I know," he said and smoothed the boy's hair.

When he released him, C.J. smiled and reached for his bike. Order had been restored.

A bike path wound through the large park. Ben led the way. Craig glanced at Jill's bike. He'd borrowed it from a neighbor. She caught him staring.

"What's so interesting about my bike?" she asked.

"I didn't know the seat went down that far." It was as far down as it would go and she still had to stretch to reach the pedals.

"We aren't all descendants of Amazons," she said tartly. "Besides, you're just jealous. Short people are superior and you tall people know it."

He laughed. "How do you figure?"

"We're ecologically superior. We take up less space, use less oxygen and don't need as much food or clothing. All that and we're just as smart and productive. There's really no reason for tall people to exist at all, but as a group, short people are very kind to those less fortunate souls.'' She smiled sweetly, then raised her chin, obviously proud of the way she talked herself out of that one.

This afternoon she wore a short-sleeved shirt tucked into stone-washed jeans. A baseball cap covered her bright red hair and sunglasses shielded her eyes.

''You don't expect anyone to believe that, do you?'' Ben asked from the front of the group.

''Yes,'' she shot back. ''You especially!''

He laughed.

Craig tried to remember the last time he'd been out like this with the boys. Recently there hadn't been a lot of fun in their lives. He had no one to blame but himself. He'd been afraid of his children and right now he couldn't figure out why.

Some of it, he admitted, was Krystal. She'd had the unique ability to make him feel inadequate. He should have recovered from her betrayals a long time ago. Maybe he had and just hadn't realized it. Maybe he was hiding behind her memory because it was easier than facing the real world.

They came out of the park at the west end. Across the street was the ice-cream store. They waited for the light, then rode across together. After leaving their bikes outside, they entered the small establishment.

There were tiny tables and chairs with round seats pushed up against the plate glass window. In the center of the store was a long refrigerator case. C.J. and Danny raced toward it and pressed their faces close, as if they had to see the contents rather than read the labels.

''I want two scoops,'' Danny said.

''Me, too.'' C.J. licked his lips. ''Rocky Road and something else.''

"Peanut butter!"

"Gross," C.J. said good-naturedly.

Craig glanced over and saw Ben and Jill having a whispered conversation. She was pointing to the display of toppings. Ben listened intently, then nodded.

Craig strolled over to join them. "What are you going to have?" he asked Jill.

"Just some yogurt," she said. "Ice cream is too rich for me."

Ten minutes later they were all seated on the benches outside. Danny had settled on a single scoop of peanut butter. C.J. had two scoops of Rocky Road topped with hot fudge. Craig had chosen strawberry ice cream, plain, while Jill was eating yogurt out of a cone. Ben came out of the store last. He had a large dish of yogurt covered with fruit and multicolored sprinkles.

"What was the secret conference about?" Craig asked.

Jill glanced at him, then at the three boys sitting on the next bench. There was a steady flow of traffic in the middle of the afternoon, and the sound of the cars kept their conversation from carrying. Even so, she lowered her voice.

"Ben wanted to know what he should have. He's sort of on a diet." She looked at her cone, then at him. While in the ice-cream shop she'd pulled off her sunglasses. Now he could see the bright green of her irises. "We've been walking every day." She laughed. "Actually, I've been walking. He's starting to run and jump and complain about how slow I am. He's taking a lunch to school and avoiding junk food. It's only been a week, but I can already see a difference."

Craig looked at his oldest, hoping she was right. Damn it, the boy deserved better than an unhappy childhood because of something as preventable as his weight. He knew it wasn't going to be an easy change, but it was possible.

"If nothing else, he seems happier," Craig said. "He's out bike riding with us. He never used to do that."

"I think he's afraid," she said. "Of being laughed at. Of being different. He wants to change but doesn't know how. He also doesn't want a fuss made." She smiled. "We have these very indirect conversations. I suppose at some point someone will have to discuss his weight with him, but so far, this plan seems to be working."

He reached out and touched her arm. "You've been good for all of us, Jill. I don't know how to thank you."

Something hot and smoky flared to life in her eyes. He told himself it was just a reflection of sunlight, but that didn't stop his sudden rush of desire. Then she blinked and her expression changed. For a moment, he thought she was going to remind him this was only temporary. He didn't want to hear that right now. He didn't want to do anything but sit here and eat his ice cream. He wanted to listen to the boys' chatter and feel that he was finally doing something right.

She gave him a quick smile. "You don't have to thank me," she said. "I'm having fun."

He leaned back on the bench and realized that for the first time in weeks, maybe months, the pain in his upper back and neck was gone. He shifted slightly, until their thighs brushed. Need spiraled up to his groin. The aching was a pleasant change from feeling nothing. He could want her without doing anything about the desire. He could admire her without making her a part of his life. He could like her and still be able to let her go.

At least that's what he was going to keep telling himself . . . for as long as it took, until the lie became truth.

## Chapter Eight

Jill could hear the baseball announcer on the television. It was about three-thirty Sunday afternoon, but despite the perfect weather, all three boys were inside, watching the game.

She paused beside the sofa. "You guys okay?" she asked.

C.J. gave her a halfhearted smile. Danny shrugged. Ben didn't bother looking at her. Craig was at the far end of the sofa, sitting on the built-in recliner, reading the Sunday paper.

"Craig?"

He glanced up at her. "Yes?"

"Do you want some popcorn or something?"

His dark eyes gave nothing away. "Sure." He returned his attention to the article he was reading.

She stood in the center of the room not sure what was going on. Yesterday had been wonderful. The five of them had spent the day together. They'd worked with Danny, gone bike riding, to the movies, then out to dinner. Afterward, they'd played cards until an hour past the boys' bedtime, because they were having such a good time. Today she felt like an unwelcome intruder spying on a secret society meeting. Signals and messages were being passed around, but she didn't know what they were. Had she done something wrong? Was everyone mad at her?

Jill tried to remember if she'd said or done something offensive the previous day, or even that morning, but she couldn't think of anything. Everyone had been fine yesterday but moody this morning.

Craig stood up and dropped the newspaper on the floor. Before she could ask him what was wrong, he brushed past her and walked up the stairs. Ben also rose to his feet and headed for the kitchen. He opened the pantry and pulled out the bag of miniature candy bars she kept for Danny and C.J.'s lunches, grabbed a handful and returned to his seat. Not once did he look at her or acknowledge her presence in the room.

"Ben, can I fix you a snack?" she asked, bewildered by his behavior. He'd been doing so well. Why was he suddenly eating candy?

He glared at her. "You're not my mother, you're just the dumb nanny. You won't even be here much longer. Quit acting like you belong and leave me alone."

Jill felt as if she'd been slapped. She didn't know whether to reprimand him or hide out in her bedroom. She settled on stunned silence. The other two boys stared at the television as if their lives depended on the outcome of the game. Ben tore off the candy wrappers and devoured the treats, one after the other.

When he was done, he got up and marched past her without saying a word.

Craig passed him on the way downstairs and entered the family room. Jill stared at him. He'd changed from jeans and a T-shirt into a dark suit and cream-colored shirt. His silk tie was dark blue with flecks of gold.

"You're going out," she said. Obviously.

Craig focused his attention on some point over her left shoulder. "I don't know when I'll be back."

"What about dinner?" she asked, feeling oddly betrayed by his behavior.

He hesitated. "I don't know when I'll be back," he repeated, and then he was gone.

What on earth was going on? Had everyone been given a script but her? She sat on the sofa and stared unseeingly at the television. What was it . . . all-males-act-like-a-jerk day? Yesterday they'd almost been a family and today she was the enemy. It wasn't fair.

Danny crawled next to her. His big eyes were filled with a questioning pain. She wanted to ask what the problem was but suddenly she didn't have the words. When he shimmied closer, she pulled him onto her lap and wrapped her arms around him. He huddled next to her like a hurt animal seeking warmth.

A few minutes later C.J. leaned against her. She settled one arm around his shoulders. Silently, they watched the rest of the game. She didn't ask what was wrong, and they didn't offer the information. When she mentioned dinner, both boys claimed not to be hungry. They went up to their rooms and closed the doors, shutting her out.

\* \* \*

Jill approached Ben's door and tapped softly. There was no answer. She turned the handle and pushed it open. Ben was asleep on his bed. She moved closer. The light on the nightstand was on, illuminating his face. She saw the tracks of tears on his skin. Her heart tightened inside her chest. She didn't know why he was hurting so she couldn't fix it.

She sat on the side of the bed and stroked his arm. He woke gradually. When he saw her, he bit his lower lip.

"I'm sorry," he mumbled, and flung himself at her.

She embraced him, feeling the awkward bones and angles of his adolescent body. He cried as if he'd lost everything dear to him. She rocked him gently, murmuring words of comfort, then sat with him until he slept again.

It was nearly nine when she made her way downstairs. Most of the lights were off. She didn't bother checking for Craig's car, so she was surprised to see him sitting in the family room. He leaned back against the sofa, his eyes closed, a drink in one hand.

He'd taken off his suit jacket and his tie. His shirt was open at the neck and the sleeves were rolled up to his elbows. She was used to seeing him in his uniform, and yesterday she'd finally convinced her heart not to flutter at the sight of him in jeans. Now she had to adjust to a completely different Craig. The successful entrepreneur. The expensive cut and material of the suit reminded her that he'd made a fortune on investments and that they really had nothing in common.

"I see you found your way back," she said. "Is everything all right?"

"You probably think we're all behaving like jerks," he said, not answering the question.

"The thought crossed my mind."

"Krystal died a year ago today."

The simple sentence caused everything to click into place. Jill sank onto the sofa and released the breath she hadn't known she'd been holding. "I'm so sorry."

"No need to be," he said, not looking at her. "I don't give a damn. But it's hard on the boys."

It was hard on him, too. She could see it in the lines on his face and the way his fingers gripped the glass, but she didn't say that.

He leaned forward and pulled open a slim drawer in the front of the end table. Under some papers was a framed photograph. He handed it to her. Jill turned it toward the light and stared at the stunning woman who had once been Craig's wife.

The photograph was several years old. Craig looked younger and there wasn't any gray at his temples. He was wearing shorts and nothing else. The woman standing next to him on the beach was tall, slender and beautiful enough to be a fashion model. Dark eyes, dark hair and a smile that promised the world. She was laughing. Involuntarily, Jill found herself wanting to smile back.

Yet, as she looked closer, she saw something cruel in the expression on Krystal's face. The set of her mouth was selfish. She didn't look like the kind of woman who would be more interested in her children than herself.

"She's very beautiful," she said carefully, handing back the picture.

Craig studied it for a moment. "Being admired was Krystal's goal in life." He set the photograph face-down on the table.

"Did you go to visit her grave?" she asked.

He nodded. "It's been a year. I started out just going for a drive, but that's where I ended up." He took a sip of his drink. "I didn't feel anything different standing there. I guess I wanted to see if there were still any ghosts. Seems like the only ones left are the ones I carry with me."

It took her a moment to realize that the bitterness on her tongue came from envy. She was envious of a dead woman. Of the power she still had over her family and the way she still possessed Craig's mind.

None of this matters, she reminded herself. Craig wasn't her man, the boys weren't her children. She was here very temporarily. But telling herself the obvious did nothing about the emotion.

"This must be very difficult for you," she said. "A year isn't all that long. You need to give yourself time to move from loving to remembering."

He turned his head and stared at her. "I haven't loved Krystal in years. If ever." He raised his glass as if toasting the photograph. "One didn't *love* Krystal, one admired and adored her. She was more interested in how things looked rather than how they really were. A tough attitude to teach children, but by God, she tried her best." His gaze narrowed. "To you, my sweet wife. May you be in the hell you deserve."

He drained his glass with one long swallow, set it next to the picture and leaned against the sofa.

"I'm sorry," Jill whispered.

"Me, too. Every damn day. That's the irony of it. I was so determined not to be like my dad." His smile was bitter. "I wasn't. Not even for a moment. It was Krystal. She could have been his twin."

"I don't understand," Jill said, before she could stop herself. She wasn't sure she wanted to hear this, but she couldn't seem to force herself to leave. Part of it was that Craig was in pain and she was at her best when someone needed her. Part of it was the man himself. She wanted to know all about him, especially his past.

"The Haynes family curse," he said. "I have five uncles and not one of them has ever been faithful to a woman. My father believed if he slept in his bed at night, he could do what he wanted the rest of the time. I swore I wouldn't be like him. I was going to be different. I wanted a wife and kids, like the old man, but I was going to be there for them. I swore fidelity, to honor and love. What a joke."

His pain was a tangible beast in the room. She could hear it breathing, clawing at him, draining his life force. She wanted to go to him and comfort him, but he wasn't Danny or C.J. He was a man, and she didn't have the right.

"I can't see you acting dishonorably," she said quietly.

"Is it honorable to be a fool?" He didn't wait for an answer, but instead continued to speak. "She was a sable-haired beauty. Now I see I wasn't thinking with my head when I met her. I was taken in by the big eyes and ready smile. I thought she was sweet and innocent. I couldn't have been more wrong. I found out later that she screwed the chauffeur who drove her to the church. They got it on right there in the back seat of the limo. After the wedding she and I drove off in the same car. And I didn't know."

Jill didn't know what to say. It was all too much to take in. Was it possible that someone could behave that horribly? She remembered what Aaron had done to her and she knew it was.

"It took me years to figure out the truth," he said, rising to his feet and crossing to the small wet bar in the far corner. "Maybe I didn't want to know what was going on. The minute I admitted it to myself, I would have had to have thrown her out. I worried about the boys and what that would do to them. I wanted so much more for them."

He uncapped a bottle of Scotch and poured about an inch into his glass. "You want some?" he asked.

"No thanks."

He leaned against the bar and stared at the empty fireplace. "In the end, she left on her own. I didn't even have the balls to throw her out. Once she was gone, she never bothered with her children. She saw them occasionally, but it was just for a few minutes at a time." He took a drink of the Scotch. "I didn't know what was right. Should I have refused to let them see her at all? Were the short visits better than nothing? Did it all confuse them?" He shrugged. "I guess I'll never know."

Dark hair fell across his forehead. She wanted to go to him and brush it away. She wanted to hold him until the pain faded and he could forget. How could Krystal have behaved like that? Didn't she know how lucky she was to have Craig? If Jill had met a man like him she would have—

She slammed the door hard on that train of thought. It was dangerous and unproductive. Krystal or no Krystal, Craig was off-limits. Jill wasn't going to get involved. This was a part-time situation.

Craig downed the last of his drink and set the glass on the bar. He swore.

"Are you more angry with her or at yourself?" she asked.

He looked at her. "Both. I hate her for what she was, and I hate myself for being such a wimp. I should have thrown her out of our lives years ago. Except then—" He shook his head. "Hell. Relationships. Do any of them work out?"

She didn't have an answer for that. She wanted them to. She believed in love—for others, if not for herself. "Some people have happy marriages," she said at last.

"Yeah. My brother Travis and his wife. And Kyle has Sandy. Austin's happy with Rebecca and if he can do it…" He walked over to the sofa and sat down. He rested his elbows on his knees and laced his hands together. "I used to think it was a family curse, but now I think it might just be me."

"Do you date much?"

He looked at her and tried to smile. The corners of his mouth tilted up, but the smile never reached his eyes. He was a beautiful, wounded male. Her heart went out to him. She wanted to touch him…heal him. Instead, she kept herself firmly in her seat.

"I don't have a lot of time. Between the boys and work." He shrugged. "Besides, I don't want to introduce them to someone until I know there's a chance that the relationship might work out. I think it would confuse them more. Sometimes it's easier to just stay home. Do you?"

"Date?" Her laugh was genuine. "No. I'm not really the dating type. And since leaving San Clemente, I haven't run into a lot of single men."

"Why do people get married?" he asked.

"Because they're in love."

"Do you believe in love?"

"Of course. Don't you?"

He drew in a breath and let it out slowly. "I'm not so sure anymore. Nothing's for sure."

"There are no guarantees, if that's what you mean, but that's not an excuse to stop trying. Eventually, there's someone out there who believes the same way and wants the same things."

"Is that love?"

"It's a part of it."

"Did you love Aaron?"

"I—" She hesitated. "I thought I did. Looking back I see that I just wanted to belong to someone, to be a part of a family. I think maybe I took the easy way out. I should have asked questions, but I didn't want to know the truth."

"Like me," he said softly.

"Yes."

The single word hung in the air and she wondered what else she'd just agreed to. Her gaze riveted on the open V of his shirt and the few dark hairs she saw. Her fingers curled toward her palms as she thought about touching him there. What would it be like?

A flush climbed her cheeks, and she looked away. The clock came into view. "Oh, it's nearly eleven," she said, shocked at how quickly the time had gone by.

Craig stood up. "I've got to be in early tomorrow. I think we're getting close on this case. Mrs. Hart is wearing a wire. A car seems to be following her, but so far no one's made a move."

"I hope it works out," she said. Before she could stand on her own, he offered his hand. She rested her fingers on his and let him pull her to her feet.

Heat radiated from him. She wanted to warm herself against him until the ice around her heart thawed. She wanted to be held in his strong arms until her strength returned.

He released her hand and smiled at her. "I always forget you're so short."

"I am not. I'm perfectly proportioned."

His smile faded. The heat moved from his body to his eyes, where she saw *and* felt the flames.

"I couldn't agree more," he said and reached for her.

She went into his embrace because the act of refusing required more strength than she possessed. His large hands spanned her back, drawing her next to him. Her fingers brushed his chest. She felt the solid muscles ripple beneath her touch.

He loomed above her, tall, powerful, masculine. Her lips trembled slightly as she anticipated what his kiss was going to feel like.

But instead of kissing her, he chuckled. "This will never work," he said.

She stiffened, prepared to pull away. "I'm sure it wasn't my idea."

Rather than releasing her, he tugged her along until he reached the end of the sofa. There he sat on the arm and spread his legs. He settled her against the apex of his thighs. They were nearly at eye level.

"Much better," he said, then covered her mouth with his.

She didn't have time to resist or think or relax or question him about anything. One moment she was wondering if she'd been insulted, the next she was being consumed by fire.

The gentle brush of his lips belied the inherent strength of his passion. She could feel it vibrating through his skin, she could smell it in the scent of his body. Inside, her heart pounded frantically. Her blood rushed, making her ears ring and her hands tremble.

He held her at her waist, his fingers brushing near her spine, his thumbs resting on her belly. Their thighs touched but not intimately. She wasn't flush against his crotch, although the thought of being there made her woman's place flare with heat.

Her hands clung to his shoulders, holding on as if she was in danger of being swept away. Just from an innocent kiss.

That's all it was. Firm lips exploring hers. He murmured her name, then kissed her again, making no effort to deepen the caress. From top to bottom, corner to corner, he discovered her lips. Then, without warning, he stroked her with his tongue.

It was as if she'd been doused by a bucket of liquid desire. From the top of her head, down to her curling toes, need swept across her skin. Her breasts swelled until her bra became an uncomfortable confinement. Her nipples hardened, then ached. Her hips arched forward, finding nothing, and her panties dampened with a sudden rush of moisture as her body prepared itself for his wondrous assault.

She parted instantly for him, admitting him into her mouth. He touched her tongue delicately with his, as if asking permission to continue. Overwhelmed by unexpected need, she clamped her lips around him and sucked.

The results were instantaneous. The hands at her waist dropped to her behind and cupped the curves, hauling her hard against him. He shifted until she was flush against him, her hot, damp need resting against the hard ridge of his arousal.

Her breasts flattened against his chest. He tilted his head and stroked his tongue against hers. She clung to him, first holding on to his shoulders, then sliding her hands down his back. Sinewy muscles rippled as if her touch could bring this large man to his knees. She arched against him, wanting it to be true, wanting more.

In response, he slipped one hand between them. His long fingers brushed against her belly, then lower, teasing her through the layers of panties and jeans. His thumb found her point of desire and he pressed there, making her whimper.

He raised his head slightly and kissed her jaw, then lower, down her neck to the collar of her shirt.

"You're incredible," he murmured against her skin. "I want to take you right here."

His words thrilled her. The hoarseness of his voice and the way his hands shook left her weak with desire.

She wanted to make love more than she'd wanted anything, but... "Craig?"

"Yeah, I know." He moved his hands back to her waist, then set her away from him. Fire still burned in his eyes, but it had been banked.

His gaze met hers. "I'm not going to apologize because I'm not sorry that happened." His smile was sheepish. "I just want you to know I don't go around seducing the boys' nannies. You're the first woman—" He cleared his throat. "No one's made me feel like this since my divorce."

"Me, either," she said, and was shocked her voice was still so breathless. Every part of her hummed with desire. She wanted him more than she wanted to be sensible. Thank goodness one of them was thinking straight.

He shifted on the sofa arm and grimaced. "You didn't sign on for this. I guess I'm saying—''

She touched her fingers to his mouth. "I know what you're saying."

Actually she didn't, but she didn't want to hear any more. If he said that this was a mistake and would never be repeated, she would be crushed. If he said it was the start of something else, she would be terrified. Better to be confused.

He bent forward and kissed her forehead. "Thanks for understanding, Jill."

Understanding what? But she didn't ask. She just stood there in the family room, long after he'd disappeared upstairs. She listened to her blood race and felt the aching need in her body. Just a couple more weeks, she told herself. Then she could walk away without looking back.

Craig was back in uniform the next morning. He joined the boys for breakfast. That was unusual, but Jill tried not to let it get to her. She ignored the way the black shirt emphasized his strength and the firm line of his freshly shaved jaw. She didn't acknowledge the secret half smile he gave her as he said, "Good morning."

"Hey, Dad," C.J. said, and handed over a box of cereal.

The boys seemed to have recovered from yesterday's upset. Except Ben. When Jill went to put a load of laundry in the washer, he followed her.

She measured in the detergent, then tossed in the whites. Socks and underwear quickly filled the machine. She set it, but didn't pull out the knob to start the cycle.

"What's wrong?" she asked, her back to the boy. She thought it would be easier for both of them to speak without actually looking at each other.

"Yesterday—"

"You've already apologized. Your dad told me about your mom. It's okay."

"I know. I just—" He moved closer. "I didn't want to eat that candy. I don't know why I did. I thought I was mad at you, and I wanted to hurt you."

She turned toward him. "Ben, that only hurts you."

He nodded, obviously miserable.

She held out her arms. He slammed against her, nearly knocking her off her feet. She leaned against the washer and absorbed his misery.

"It was just a mistake," she said as she smoothed his hair. "You'll do better today."

"But we didn't go for a walk."

"I didn't know if you'd want to."

He raised his head. Tears swam in his eyes. "I did."

"We'll go tomorrow. I promise."

He swiped at his face with the back of his hand. "Okay."

"Let's go get some breakfast."

He walked with her to the table. Craig glanced at her, but she smiled to tell him everything was fine.

"I thought I'd take you boys to school today."

"Cool," Danny said. "Dibs on front."

"It's my turn," C.J. said.

Danny stuck out his lower lip but didn't argue.

Jill started making Ben's lunch.

The conversation flowed behind her. She liked mornings with the boys. As long as they weren't fighting, they were great fun to be with. Craig's voice traveled across the kitchen and set her nerves to quivering. She worked quickly so she didn't have to think about what had happened—and not happened—between them last night.

"Jill, are you leaving soon?" Danny asked.

She looked at the boy. "What do you mean?"

"Yesterday Ben said you were gonna be going. Are you leaving us?"

All three boys stared accusingly at her.

"When I started, I told you I was just staying until spring break."

"But that was before," Ben said. "You can't go."

"Jill has her own life to think of," Craig said. "Leave her alone. Which reminds me. I've got to start interviewing nannies."

Another nanny? The thought should have thrilled her, but instead she felt vaguely unsettled. She wasn't ready to move on.

C.J. pushed his cereal bowl away. "It's too soon, Jill."

"Stay," Ben said.

"I have a job," she said. "My condo is only sublet until September. I really can't...." But she didn't know what she couldn't do.

"Then stay until then," C.J. said. "Until September. We can spend the summer together."

"We'll have the best time!" Danny promised. He scrunched up his nose. "Please?"

Her throat tightened, making it difficult to swallow. It wasn't supposed to be like this. She wasn't supposed to get involved.

She glanced at Craig. "I haven't set up any interviews," he said. "I'd love for you to stay. But it's your decision."

Staying was risky. Not just because Craig reduced her to putty in his arms, but because of the boys. She was foolish to think she could hold her heart at bay.

September. That was over five months away. Five months was a long time. She could figure out what she wanted to do with her life. So far she hadn't given that a thought. Staying here would allow her to finish healing and then plan things out.

Could she take the chance? She stared at the three boys. Could she walk away from them now, when they were just figuring out how to live together?

"All right," she said. "I'll stay until September."

There was a collective cheer. C.J. and Danny raced over and hugged her. Craig stood up. "Thanks, Jill. I really appreciate this." He glanced at his children. "We'd better get going."

The boys started for the door. Ben came back and reached for the lunch sack she was holding out. He hesitated, then bent down and kissed her cheek.

"Way cool," he said.

She watched him walk away and knew she'd just given up another chunk of her heart. How long until Danny and Craig took the rest?

## Chapter Nine

"**Y**ou can't go on the teacups. You'll throw up," Ben said with the superiority of the older brother who has experienced life.

Danny's lower lip quivered. "I can too go on the ride, and I won't throw up. You're just a fat old mobyhead!"

Ben lunged for Danny. C.J. stuck out a foot and nearly tripped him. Danny started to cry.

"Boys, it looks to me as if everyone is a little tired," Jill said. "Maybe we should all go back to the room and take a nap."

"No way!" Ben said.

"Jill, come on, *I* wasn't doing anything wrong," C.J. told her.

"I don't want to take a nap." Danny wiped his face with the back of his hand.

Craig put his arm around her shoulders and grinned. "I'd like to take this moment to remind you that I did offer you the week off. You're the one who got excited and declared that you hadn't been to Disneyland in years."

She laughed as she glanced up at him. "Everyone gets to make one mistake."

As he winked, her stomach tightened slightly and she had to fight to keep her toes from curling inside her athletic shoes. "Okay, here's how it goes. Ben, you and C.J. get one of the cups and your dad, Danny and I will take another." She glanced at the youngest Haynes. "Danny, if you throw up, I'm going to be very unhappy."

"I won't," he promised and leaned against her. The line moved forward as the brightly colored teacups the size of large dining-room tables twirled and spun on a rapidly spinning base.

She'd agreed to come with the boys and their father to Disneyland for the reason she'd told Craig. She *hadn't* been here in years. In addition, she was concerned about Ben. He'd been on his low-fat, more-exercise program for a month and was doing great. However, a week at an amusement park could be a lot of temptation for a twelve-year-old boy. The last reason, the one she admitted only to herself, and only in the privacy of her hotel room late at night when she couldn't sleep, was that she wanted to know what Craig was like when he wasn't so caught up in work.

It was a delicious form of torture. He was far too good-looking for a mere mortal man. Her heart was in a constant state of excitement; her palms sweated on an alarmingly regular basis. If she didn't know better, she would think she was coming down with some deadly tropical disease. But it wasn't anything that interesting. Only attraction to her boss. A condition so common, it was a cliché.

Not that anything had happened between them. There had been that one kiss, then nothing. It was as if by agreeing to stay with the boys through the end of summer, she'd reminded him of her position in his house. He hadn't made another move. No matter how often she'd silently willed him to.

The line moved forward again. The boys talked with one another. This was their second day at the park. They'd driven down in two easy days, stopping at several places along the way. They'd spent the night in a resort just north of Santa Barbara. For the first time, she'd seen proof of Craig's financial resources. He'd put himself and the boys up in a two-bedroom suite, complete with a stunning view of the mountains and a whirlpool bath that could float a battalion. Her room across the hall had been equally lovely, with a king-size bed, a sitting area and a pretty impressive tub of its own. She'd protested the expense, but Craig had just laughed.

Now they were staying at the Disneyland Hotel. The sleeping arrangements were repeated. She had a mini-suite across the hall. After a long day of rides and adventures, it was nice to stretch out in the quiet. Occasionally, she wished for something more—someone to turn to, someone to hold her. If she made the mistake of closing her eyes and visualizing herself with someone, he always looked exactly like Craig.

"We're next!" Ben shouted. The young man monitoring the ride motioned him to a cup on the far side. Ben and C.J. took off running.

"We're together," Craig said, pointing at Danny, then at her.

"Right over here, sir," the attendant said.

The three of them walked toward the cup. Danny danced around them. "Can we go really fast? Can we spin so fast we fly away? Can we spin faster than Ben and C.J.? You think I'm gonna throw up?"

Jill ruffled his hair. "Yes, we'll go fast, and, no, you're not going to throw up."

She slipped into the cup and sat. Danny was next to her, Craig across from her. The area was tight. Their knees bumped.

"What do we do?" Danny asked.

Craig placed the boy's hands on the plate-size disk sticking up from the center of the cup. "Once the ride starts, turn this as fast as you can. We'll spin around."

Danny bounced in his seat. "How do you know when the ride starts?"

Jill leaned close and grinned. "The floor starts moving."

"Really?"

Faint freckles stretched across his nose. She'd had the boys' hair cut before they left, so his bangs didn't fall all the way to his eyes. Like Craig and herself, he was dressed in jeans and a short-sleeved shirt. The Southern California spring weather was perfect. Clear skies, balmy days, cool nights. It was the stuff travel videos were made of.

Suddenly the cup began to move.

"Now!" Craig said and reached for the control in the center of the cup. Jill grabbed it, too. They turned together, pulling their teacup around.

Danny forgot to help. He was too busy staring at everything. He spotted his brothers and screamed with delight. "We're going faster!"

Ben and C.J. were hunched over, working frantically to turn their cup. Others around them swirled and spun until the area was a mass of wildly rotating teacups.

Jill laughed. She looked up and saw the beautiful merry-go-round spinning out of sight. She had a view of other rides and blurry people before her attention focused on Craig.

In an effort to keep the cup turning, they both spun the control. Their hands constantly brushed and overlapped. His skin was dry and warm, his fingers strong. Since arriving at the park, there had been a lot of touching. He often draped his arm around her while they were standing in line for rides. She'd held hands with him as they'd made their way through the crowd after the parade the previous night. Bodies had brushed on various rides.

If she was foolish, she would allow herself to believe this was all real. She might even start to picture herself staying in Craig's home. But that wasn't going to happen. This wasn't her family, he wasn't her man. She was still on the outside, looking in.

The ride slowed. When it stopped, Danny scrambled out and raced to his brothers. "I didn't throw up once, and we went faster than you."

"Brat," Ben said good-naturedly and spun Danny around. The boy shrieked with laughter.

Craig glanced at his watch. "I'm starving. Where should we go for lunch? I'd say fast food, but I don't want to do that to Ben." He stared at his oldest. "I can't believe the change in him. It's only been a month, but he looks like a different kid.''

Jill followed his gaze. The weight was falling off the boy. Between the low-fat food and his increased activities, he was becoming a new person.

"I know what you mean," she said. "All his clothes were hanging on him. We had to buy new jeans for this trip."

"It's not just how he looks. He seems to be enjoying life more. He's always running and jumping, and he's a hell of a lot more fun to be around. He looks happy."

"Yeah." She smiled. "A few more pounds, and he'll be nearly as good-looking as his father."

The words came out of her mouth without warning. She wanted to call them back, but it was too late. They hung there between them, loud and obvious.

Jill clamped her hand over her mouth and blushed. She could feel the heat climbing her cheeks to her hairline.

She risked glancing at Craig. He raised his eyebrows. "What I meant," she said, then cleared her throat. "That is—"

He silenced her with a quick shake of his head. "I don't want to hear what you meant, lady. I like what you said just fine."

"I bet," she grumbled.

"For what it's worth, you're not half-bad yourself."

"Gee, thanks. Not half-bad. I live for compliments like that."

He smiled at her, but the fire in his eyes spoke of something else. Something tempting and potentially dangerous. She didn't dare indulge, but if he asked, it was going to be hard to say no.

She searched her mind for a safe topic that would change the subject. "C.J. looks a lot like you, too," she said brightly. "Only Danny is different. He must take after his mother."

Instead of answering, Craig called for the boys, then returned his attention to her. "Let's head back to the hotel," he said. "We can use the rest, and there will be more choices, food-wise."

"Good idea." She glanced at him out of the corner of her eye. If she wasn't mistaken, she'd upset Craig. But how? By saying Danny looked like his mother? She squeezed her eyes shut and fought back a groan. After all Craig had told her about Krystal, it wasn't surprising that he didn't want to be reminded of her. Dumb, Bradford, really dumb.

She touched his arm. "Sorry," she said softly.

He stared at her for a moment, then dropped his arm around her shoulders and pulled her close. "Don't apologize," he said, brushing his lips against the top of her head. "You didn't do anything wrong. Let's go eat."

They headed for the monorail that would take them back to the hotel. Craig kept his arm around her shoulders, although Danny ducked between them. C.J. took his father's other hand, and Ben surprised her by grabbing her arm and hanging on. It was a perfect moment and she wanted it to last forever.

"More wine?" Craig asked, holding up the bottle.

Jill glanced at him, then shyly averted her eyes. "Sure," she said, holding out her glass.

He poured the pale liquid, then set the bottle back into the portable ice bucket next to the table. Candlelight flickered from all the tables. In the corner, a small four-piece combo provided soft music, and several couples filled the small square of dance floor next to them.

He drew in a deep breath and raised his glass. "To the peace and quiet."

She smiled. "Without the boys around, I'm not sure I'll know what to do with myself."

He wanted to tell her he would think of something. Just staring at her brought several suggestions to mind. But he didn't voice them. They hadn't even had the salad yet. However, the lack of food didn't keep him from wanting her.

Women's ability to transform themselves had always amazed him, and Jill was no exception. This afternoon she'd been funny and charming in jeans and a white shirt that shouldn't have been sexy but was. She'd worn athletic shoes and a Goofy hat, complete with floppy ears. She'd eaten cotton candy with Ben, ridden the scariest rides without flinching and had generally been one of the guys.

Tonight, just a couple of hours later, she was every man's fantasy. Her hair looked casually tousled, with a few wisps falling on her forehead. Makeup deepened her green irises until they glowed like emeralds. She wore a dress that matched her eyes. The silky green fabric clung to her curves in a way that made his mouth water. The deep scoop neck gave him a glimpse of creamy breasts. Except for a delicate gold chain around her wrist, her arms were bare. She swayed in time with the music and he was mesmerized.

If only she wasn't so damn small. As he studied her, he couldn't help but picture her naked...in bed... wanting him. But that's as far as his imagination went. Would he hurt her? If he forgot himself in the heat of the moment, could his weight crush her? He'd had his share of lovers when he'd been in college, and they'd all been tall women, with long legs and torsos. Feminine, but not fragile. And *fragile* was the word he used when he thought of Jill.

It's not going to be a problem because you're not going to do anything, he reminded himself. He was taking her out for a nice dinner to thank her for all she'd done on this trip. Also, because he liked being alone with her. But it wasn't a romantic rendezvous, no matter how much he wanted it to be.

She took a sip of wine and sighed.

"What's wrong?" he asked.

"I'm just worried about the boys. Do you think they're all right?"

He laughed. "They're in a huge suite with unlimited junk food, cable TV and a baby-sitter who was pretty enough to play Cinderella in the parade. I think they're really happy."

"Well, if you put it like that." She glanced up at him. "I'm having a wonderful time, Craig. Thanks for inviting me."

"Thank you for coming with us. It wasn't part of your job description."

"I know, but what would I have done if I'd stayed behind? With you and the boys gone, I would have had too much time on my hands."

The waiter approached and set their salads in front of them. Craig thanked him and picked up his fork. "So what do you think of the Magic Kingdom?"

"It's wonderful. No matter how old I get, I always have a wonderful time at Disneyland."

"Good. I thought we'd spend most of tomorrow on Tom Sawyer's Island."

"Do I get to be an Indian?" she asked, her eyes glowing with amusement.

Heat seared through him, sparking an arousal that threatened his composure. "You get to be anything you want."

They ate in silence for a few minutes. The quiet wasn't uncomfortable. In addition to finding her damned attractive, Craig thought Jill was easy to be around. She didn't expect a lot of chatter or mind if the conversation strayed from her interests. In fact, he thought, frowning, she rarely talked about herself. He didn't know very much about her at all.

"I never thought to ask," he said. "Is being here bringing up memories of your stepchildren?"

She glanced up, obviously startled. "No. I never thought about it. I'm sure Aaron and I brought the girls here, but I don't remember much about our visit. I guess it wasn't very memorable."

"He has two girls?"

She nodded.

"Are they really different from boys?"

She grinned. "Let's put it this way. Patti and Heather never had a farting contest in the car, or anywhere else for that matter."

The waiter returned and cleared their plates. The combo started another song—a slow and sultry number that made him long to be close to her.

"Dance?" he asked, rising to his feet and holding out his hand.

She hesitated. "I'm not very good."

"Neither am I."

She took his hand and allowed him to lead her to the tiny floor. Several other couples were already there, swaying to the music. There wasn't room to do anything fancy, and he was grateful. He just wanted to hold Jill in his arms and torture himself into mindlessness.

She was wearing high heels and her head nearly cleared his shoulders. He placed one hand on the small of her back and linked his other with hers. Three inches separated them. He waited until they'd found their rhythm together before drawing her closer.

He'd thought she might resist the contact, but she flowed against him like water over stone, molding herself to his body. Her curves teased him. Through his suit jacket and shirt, he felt the soft imprint of her breasts. Her breath heated his skin and her legs brushed against his.

They took small steps, circling with the other dancers, not talking but absorbing the sounds and sensations. Without thinking, he released her fingers and pressed both his hands against her back. She was fine-boned and all woman. Need rocketed through him. She fanned the desire when she slipped her hands under his jacket and hugged his waist.

Their breathing became synchronized, their steps, smaller. With the slightest hint from her, he would have carried her back to her hotel room and made love with her until they were both too exhausted to do more than cling to each other. But she didn't hint and he didn't offer. So when the song ended, they parted, clapping politely, and he led her toward their table.

They passed an elderly couple. The woman smiled at him. "You and your wife are very lovely together. Are you celebrating an anniversary?"

"No," he said, thinking it would be too much trouble to correct their false impression.

She winked. "Maybe not tonight, but my guess is you'll be celebrating many, many more."

"Thank you." He nodded and placed his hand on Jill's back. She moved forward, then slipped into her chair before he could pull it out for her.

She was quiet for the rest of the meal. She didn't meet his gaze, and when the main course came, she only ate a small amount.

"Did you like your dinner?" he asked when the waiter took away her nearly full plate.

"It was delicious. I just wasn't hungry."

"Why?"

She glanced around. "Can we leave, please?"

"Sure." He signaled for the check.

In a matter of moments, he'd charged the meal to the room and followed her outside. A dull ache began at the base of his neck and worked its way down to his shoulder blades.

"Jill, what's wrong?" he asked.

There were several couples standing outside the restaurant. She shook her head and started walking. Just past the dancing fountains was a small wooden bench, partially hidden by the lush foliage. She sank down onto the seat.

"Jill?"

She stared up at him, her eyes twin pools of confusion. Without thinking, he settled next to her, gathered her in his arms and kissed her.

Her mouth was as soft and sweet as he remembered. Her lips parted instantly and he touched the delicate surface of her tongue. She responded by clinging to him. Their breathing increased. The steady throbbing between his legs quickened to an unbearable cadence of pulsing pressure.

He moved his hands over her back, tracing a line from her spine to her derriere, then cupping her hips. Before he moved higher and touched her breasts, she broke away.

"Stop," she said hoarsely. "You must stop."

"Why?"

Her laughter had a sharp edge. "Because I'm not doing this again."

"What are you talking about?"

She moved back on the bench until they weren't touching at all. Her face was in shadows; only her eyes were lit by the lights along the path in front of them. She rested her hands on her lap. She seemed calm, even relaxed. Only her fingers betrayed her as they twisted together.

"This isn't right. At least it's not right for me." She cleared her throat. "I can't do this again."

"Do what?"

"Be used. All my life men have used me."

He stiffened. He wanted to protest that he hadn't used her, but sensed this wasn't really about him. "What do you mean?"

"Men have used me to get what they want. They've never cared about me. My father used me to upset my mother, before and after the divorce. My stepfather pretended to be my friend in front of other people, but when we were alone, he told me I was stupid and ugly and that he didn't like me at all."

"Bastard," Craig growled, wishing he could find the man and beat him into a whining, bleeding pulp.

"Then Aaron used me in the biggest way possible. We had mutual friends, and he knew that my goal in life was to be a part of a family. When we started dating, he used that against me. He talked about the girls and how much they needed a mother in their lives. I was too ignorant to realize they already had one. I bought his story, married him, moved in and proceeded to support the entire family."

She closed her eyes and drew in a deep breath. "After a couple of years I wanted a baby of my own. Aaron was against the idea. He already had two children, he didn't want any more."

"I'm sorry," he said softly. Bitterness filled his mouth. All three of his boys had been accidents. Krystal hadn't wanted children, either. Aaron was a complete jerk if he didn't know what a treasure he'd had in Jill.

"I kept after him about a baby, and he finally agreed. We tried for six months, but nothing happened." She looked at him. Her mouth trembled, but she spoke clearly. "I wanted to go to a doctor, but he said we should keep trying. Then his ex-wife sued for custody of the girls."

"You don't have to tell me this," he said.

"Yes, I do. I want you to know why I feel the way I do." She shifted on the seat, turning toward him. "Once the court proceedings started, we both agreed it would be silly for me to get pregnant now. I went back on the Pill. When we lost the custody battle, Aaron was furious. I tried to comfort him."

Her hands twisted together frantically. He leaned forward and covered her fingers with his. She clutched his hand as if it were a lifeline. Her dark gaze locked on his. His heart ached for her. No one should have to suffer this much for anyone, least of all a creep like Aaron.

"We were still in the courtroom," she continued. "His ex-wife was laughing and hugging the girls. I tried to hold him, but he pushed me away. I remember crying. I was devastated. I told Aaron we could still have a baby of our o-own." Her voice cracked.

"She looked at me, then—Aaron's ex-wife. She stared at me with pity and called me a fool. There in front of the judge and everyone, she told me that Aaron had had a vasectomy years ago. Right after Heather was born. So unless he'd had it reversed, there wasn't going to be another baby."

Craig swore loudly. The urge to violence nearly overwhelmed him. That piece of— He swore again. Jill didn't seem to hear him. She kept on talking.

"Aaron just looked away. He didn't say a word. When I asked him if it was true, he just shrugged, like it didn't matter. The girls ignored me, too. As if I'd never existed for them. All those years had meant nothing. That week Aaron told me he would have his attorney draw up the divorce papers."

She started to shake. Craig didn't know whether to pull her close or leave her alone. She settled the matter by releasing her hands and folding her arms over her chest.

"I never saw him again. I never spoke to him. I don't know if I would have wanted to save the marriage or not, but I didn't get the chance to decide. I gave him and his daughters everything I had, and they never gave anything back. I suppose I'm a fool for taking it all those years. But I just wanted to belong. For once in my life, I wanted to be a part of a family.''

Her story stunned him. It was too much to absorb. He knew there were bastards in the world; his father was one of the biggest. How had Jill hooked up with so many? She deserved more.

"Jill, I'm not Aaron."

"I know, but even if you were, it doesn't matter. I'm not going to be used again. I'm not going to be taken advantage of just because I'm convenient. I'm here to look after your children, and that's all I want to do. I can't afford to get involved with you. It's too much like what just happened to me. It would be too easy to fall for you. I don't want to get hurt again."

He wanted to protest. It wouldn't have to be like that. He and Jill had a powerful attraction between them. Maybe—

Maybe what? He, of all people, should understand her concerns. He was a little gun-shy himself. He was only interested in a sure thing and life didn't come with guarantees. Was he willing to promise her exactly what she needed? He already knew the answer to that. They were both too wounded for a relationship between them to work.

"You're right," he said. "I'm sorry."

"Don't apologize. This was all pretty wonderful. I'm not ungrateful or angry. I just finally figured this out, and I wanted to be honest with you." Her smile trembled a little at the corners, but he wasn't going to comment on the fact.

"I appreciate that," he said.

He wanted more, though. He wanted it all. Damn the consequences, there was something about Jill that appealed to him. But he couldn't force it. Besides, he was forgetting who was important here. It wasn't him, it was the boys. They'd been through so much. They deserved better. Right now, Jill was the best part of their lives. They didn't need him messing that up for them.

"I still want to apologize," he told her. "Frankly, I want to find Aaron and your stepfather and beat them both up."

"Thank you for that. I wouldn't mind watching."

They stared at each other. He wondered if she felt as awkward as he did. Even if he couldn't have a relationship with her, he wanted her to stay for the boys. How did he tell her that?

"Friends?" he said at last, holding out his hand.

She hesitated for a moment, then took it in hers. "Friends," she agreed.

Friends, he thought. Why did the word sound so empty?

## Chapter Ten

On the way to Disneyland, the miles had seemed to fly by, but on the way home, they crawled. Jill caught herself staring at the speedometer for the third time that hour. The needle was still set at sixty-five. She supposed they must really be going that fast, but it didn't feel like it. She just wanted to get back to the house so she could escape to her room.

The radio played softly but the sad country music didn't do anything to improve her mood. There wasn't even arguing from the boys to distract her. They'd gotten an early start so they could make the drive back in one day. The boys were dozing in the back seat. Danny had barely stirred enough to eat breakfast.

Jill stared out the side window and fought down a sigh. She wanted to offer to drive, but she and Craig had traded off less than a half hour ago. She closed her eyes and willed herself to be anywhere but here.

It was her own fault. She knew better, but she'd done it anyway. She'd withdrawn from Craig and the boys, and now they all knew something was wrong.

She'd caught Craig studying her when he thought she didn't see. The boys had all stared at her with their soulful eyes full of pain and questions. She'd thought about explaining, but what was there to say?

She should never have let Craig take her to dinner. She should never have agreed to that dance, or responded to his kiss. She should never have told him the truth.

Every time she thought about what she'd said, embarrassment flooded her body. Her face got hot, her palms dampened, and she felt like the world's biggest fool. How could she have let Aaron treat her like that? How could she have willingly admitted it to Craig? Thinking about the past didn't make her angry, it made her feel worthless.

It had been the night, she told herself. When he'd kissed her, she'd wanted him so much. She'd wanted it to be real. All of it. Not just his affection, but the boys' feelings, too. She liked taking care of them. She liked being the one they confessed their secrets to, the one they ran to when they were hurt. She even liked that they felt secure enough to get mad at her. After years of being lonely, her heart responded to the love between the boys and their father. She wanted a piece of that for herself. Was that so wrong?

She knew the answer. Of course it wasn't wrong. It also wasn't real. She was just the hired help. Craig was doing exactly what Aaron did, only Craig was being honest. He paid her for her services, gave her a title and time off if she wanted it. She'd known the risks when she'd taken the job. She shifted on her seat. That wasn't completely true. There was one risk she hadn't considered.

Craig.

What was she going to do about him? When he held her in his arms, she wanted to surrender all to him. She wanted to be with him, touch him, feel him against her, in her. He made her feel safe and cared for. He was the kind of man a woman dreamed about marrying. He was a fantasy come to life. Good-looking, honest, intelligent, funny, loving and sexy enough to melt pure steel, let alone her lonely woman's heart.

That made it worse—being so close to what she could never have. She still believed in love, just not for herself. Somehow, she always came out on the losing end of her romantic relationships.

For some people, things just sort of worked out. Kim had found Brian. They were deeply in love. It hadn't worked out for Craig, she reminded herself. Krystal had nearly destroyed him. They were two wounded souls. What did that mean? Should they try to find comfort together, or should they run like hell before they got hurt again?

Her first instinct was to run. She wanted to open the car door, jump out and run as fast and as far away as possible. She glanced over her shoulder at the boys. They were all dozing. She couldn't abandon them unexpectedly. They'd already been through so much. She would have to find her way to make peace with her feelings about Craig. How hard could that be? After her confession a few days ago, she'd made it clear she wasn't interested in a personal relationship. Craig was too much of a gentleman not to honor her request.

The realization should have made her happy. It should have made her able to relax. It didn't. Instead, she found herself counting the mile markers and wishing she had the courage to try again.

They returned home to a musty house and a flashing answering machine. Jill instructed the boys to carry their bags upstairs. Ben and C.J. hauled their stuff up immediately. Danny sat at the bottom of the stairs and stared listlessly at her.

"I don't feel good," he said.

Jill frowned. He'd been quiet the whole way home. Too quiet. She touched his face. It was warm. "You might have a fever. Where's the thermometer?"

He shrugged. His light brown hair stuck to his forehead in sweaty patches.

Craig brought in another load of luggage. He paused. "What's the problem?"

"I think Danny's sick," she said.

He came over and looked at his son. "He's got a fever. How long have you felt bad?" he asked.

Danny shrugged again. "Last night, maybe."

Craig took the stairs two at a time. He returned with a thermometer, which he rinsed at the sink before sticking it into Danny's mouth. The boy obligingly clamped his tongue over it and leaned against the railing.

C.J. came downstairs and looked at him. "What's wrong with him?"

"I'm not sure," Jill said, bending over and touching Danny's face again. "Maybe it's just from the trip."

C.J. walked into the family room and stopped in front of the answering machine. "There's a message, Dad."

"Go ahead and play it."

Jill expected it to be someone from the station, but instead a woman identified herself as a teacher from Danny's school. "Mr. Haynes, one of Danny's classmates has come down with chicken pox. The incubation on that is about fourteen to twenty-one days, so he will probably get sick sometime during the spring break. I'm sorry to be the bearer of such bad news." There was a pause and the sound of ruffling papers. The voice continued.

"I see here you have two other boys. If they haven't been exposed, you're going to have to expect the worst. Call me if you need any more information." She left her number, then hung up.

Jill stared at Craig. "Tell me C.J. and Ben have already been exposed."

"They haven't."

She looked down at Danny. Chicken pox times three. The teacher had been right about expecting the worst. She removed the thermometer and studied it. "Just a hair over a hundred. You have a fever, my man. Can you make it up the stairs to your bed?"

Before he could answer, Craig picked him up and carried him. Jill glanced at C.J. "Enjoy your last few days of health."

"I won't get 'em," he said confidently.

"Uh-huh. No one asks you your opinion. This stuff is very contagious. Look at it this way. You'll miss school, lay around and watch TV all day, and I'll try to tempt you to eat with pudding and ice cream."

C.J. grinned. "All right!"

"We'll see how you like it when it happens," she said, and moved into the kitchen. She put a call into the children's pediatrician to find out if there was anything she needed to be aware of, then sat at the table and wrote out a shopping list. She was preparing for a siege. About the time Danny was feeling better, C.J. and Ben would start getting sick. She figured it was going to be about three weeks of hell.

Craig came into the kitchen. "I put Danny in bed. He says he just wants to sleep."

She looked up from her list. "It's probably the best thing for him. I've put a call in to the doctor. There's some children's medication on the top shelf. That should help his fever."

"I'll take it up to him." He ran his hand through his hair. "They've been inoculated against just about everything else. I'm sorry this had to happen while you were here. I can see if the station will let me extend my vacation."

She shook her head. "Don't be silly. You had enough trouble getting the days off to take the boys to Disneyland. If you hadn't arranged it months ago, you couldn't have done it at all. We'll be fine. Danny will be up and feeling better before C.J. or Ben gets it. By then, I'll be an expert."

"And exhausted."

"Maybe, but I can always sleep later." She gave him a half smile. "Can you take care of things here while I run to the grocery store? I want to lay in supplies."

"Sure." He followed her out to the garage. "The timing is really bad on this."

"There's no good time for kids to be sick."

"I know, but—"

She paused and glanced at him. Despite the long drive, the lines of weariness by his eyes and the stubble darkening his jaw, he was still good-looking enough to make her heart pound as if she'd just endured an advanced step-aerobics class. Worse, she knew what he was thinking.

"I'm not leaving," she said softly.

He shoved his hands in his front jeans pockets. "You've thought about it."

He had her there. "Yes, it crossed my mind. But I agreed to take this job, and I don't turn my back on my responsibilities."

"I don't want you to stay if you don't want to be here."

"I know." She stared at the concrete floor of the garage, then glanced back at him. "It's not that simple, Craig. You know that. Part of me is scared. I like the boys, being with them, with you. Being part of this family. It's all I've ever wanted. But it's temporary. I can't let myself get emotionally involved."

"If it's that complicated, maybe you should leave. I don't want you getting hurt."

His concern was bittersweet. There was a part of her that appreciated his willingness to sacrifice for her, while the rest of her was wounded that he would consider letting her go without a fight. Her conflict only proved how terribly confused she was by the situation.

"I think I need to stay," she said. "Not just because I gave my word, but because I have something to prove to myself. I need to be able to do this and then walk away."

"What if we don't want you to go?"

We. What we? The boys? Him and the boys? Or just him?

"I don't have an answer for that," she said. "I'm sorry about what happened when we were away. I shouldn't have sent out such mixed signals."

"It's my fault," he said quickly.

"Stop being such a nice guy. It wasn't your fault. Or maybe we're equally to blame. I knew going to dinner was a mistake, but I wanted to do it anyway because—" She ducked her head, fighting a heat flaring on her cheeks.

"Because there's an obvious attraction between us." His voice was low and husky.

"Something like that."

"Exactly like that." He moved closer and touched his forefinger to her chin, forcing her to look at him. His dark eyes blazed with fire again. The heat warmed her from the inside out. Her breasts swelled, and her thighs began to tremble.

"What makes it scary for both of us is that it's more than just sexual attraction," he said. "We happen to like each other, too."

The blush on her cheeks deepened. "How can you even talk about it?"

"How can we not? Silence won't make it go away. If I can't trust you with this conversation, Jill, what's the point of having the feelings?"

He terrified her. The urge to run was stronger than any passionate fire. She wanted to bolt for freedom and safety. Craig was everything she'd ever wanted in a man. He was honest enough to make her squirm.

He brushed his thumb across her mouth. She wanted to taste his skin. She wanted to pull him close and kiss him. She needed to get away.

"Let it go," he said. "Stop thinking about it. We're both carrying around a lot of misery from our pasts. We don't have to make any decisions today."

That sounded simple enough, but how was she supposed to shut down her brain?

"I have to get to the grocery store," she said. "And you should check on Danny."

This time she gave in to the urge to run. She half jogged to the car, then backed out of the driveway quickly. Stop thinking about it, she thought, grimacing. Yeah, right. How was she supposed to do that?

Two weeks and six days later Jill had her answer. Exhaustion. A person could forget anything if she was exhausted enough. She sank into the kitchen chair and listened to the blissful silence. Danny and Ben were at school and C.J. was upstairs, playing video games and listening to his radio.

She'd barely finished nursing Danny through the fever and itchy rash when Ben had come down with chicken pox. Two days later, C.J. had a fever and the first hint of red on his back. She'd played board games, rented videos, made enough Jell-O and pudding to float a small armada. She'd tempted their appetites with homemade bread, an assortment of soups, rice pudding and Popsicles. She'd forced liquids down their throats, held them when they cried, was patient when they whined and generally used up every single bit of strength she had.

C.J. would probably go back to school tomorrow, then she could get on with her regular routine. The first thing she wanted to do was catch up on her sleep.

Jill rubbed her eyes. They were gritty from long nights up with the boys. Craig had helped out as much as he could, but they'd had a break in the case and he'd had to go help make three arrests. That last guy was still at large, but the elderly citizens were no longer in danger of being hurt or swindled. Last night, Mrs. Hart had sent over a large chocolate cake to say thank you. Everyone had enjoyed a slice of it except Jill. She glanced at it now, sitting on the counter. It didn't tempt her at all, which was odd. She loved chocolate.

She rose to her feet and walked to the bottom of the stairs. Everything hurt. Her legs, her arms, her head, even her hair was throbbing in time with her pulse.

"C.J.," she called.

"Yeah?"

"I'm going to take a nap. Wake me up when you want lunch."

"Okay, Jill."

She thought about going into her bedroom, but suddenly it was just too far away. The sofa was closer. The plump cushions looked inviting. She would just lay her head down for a moment.

The next thing she knew, strong arms were lifting her up in the air. Everything was very surreal, fading in and out. Sounds gurgled, as if she were underwater. She blinked and focused on a familiar face.

"Craig?" she asked. Her voice was a whisper. She cleared her throat to speak louder, but it didn't help.

"Hush," he told her. "I've got you. I'm putting you to bed." His arms tightened slightly. "Why the hell didn't you tell me you hadn't been exposed to chicken pox?"

"Huh?" She tried to raise her head, but it was too much effort. "Chicken pox? Didn't I have them when I was little? I don't remember."

"No, you didn't, because you've got them now." He placed her on the bed.

The sheets felt cool against her heated skin, especially when he pulled off her T-shirt and jeans. His strong hands reached behind her and unfastened her bra.

"I'm naked," she whispered in wonder.

"Just about." He stuck her hands into the short sleeves of the oversized T-shirt she wore to bed, then pulled it down to her waist.

"Did you look?"

He chuckled. "You're delirious with fever, if you have to ask. Of course I looked. I'm a guy. Put this under your tongue."

She opened her mouth obediently as he placed the thermometer in her mouth. She watched him fold her clothes. The edges of the room seemed to be blurring.

"I called the doctor," he said. "We have to watch you. The big concern is fever. We have to keep that down. You're going to have to drink a lot of liquids. Can you do that?"

She thought about nodding, but it took too much effort. She fluttered her fingers instead.

He pulled the thermometer out of her mouth. "A hundred and one. Damn." He eased her down on the mattress. "Try to sleep, Jill. I'm going to be right here."

She closed her eyes, then opened them again. "Danny, Ben. I have to pick them up."

"I'll take care of it. You just concentrate on getting well."

He squeezed her hand, then bent over and kissed her forehead. "I'm really sorry about this, Jill."

"S'okay." She wanted to ask him to kiss her again. She'd liked the feel of his lips on hers. She would tell him. Just as soon as she opened her eyes.

Although the thought stayed in her mind, she never got around to mentioning it. When she next surfaced, the room was dark, and Craig was dozing in a chair beside her bed. He must have heard her stirring. He came awake instantly and smiled.

"Feel like drinking something?"

"Sure."

Her throat was dry, and she could barely talk. She made a move to sit up. The second her legs brushed against the sheets, she realized her skin was one hot, burning itch.

"Oh, my Lord," she said and threw back the sheets.

A rash covered her from the tips of her toes to the tops of her thighs. She stared at it in the dim light. She could make out tiny bumps. She had to curl her fingers into her palms to keep from scratching.

Craig sucked in his breath. "It looks bad."

She realized it was on her back, her belly, her arms. "It's everywhere," she said miserably, desperately wanting to rub against the sheets but knowing she shouldn't. Tears sprang to her eyes.

"Oh, honey, don't," Craig said, sliding off the chair and onto the floor. He knelt beside her and held out his arms. She threw herself against him and whimpered.

"Hush," he murmured. "We'll use ice and lotion. The doctor gave you a prescription to help with the itching, too. You'll be okay."

She realized he wasn't holding her. Because she was hideous looking, she thought, even as a rational part of her whispered that he was probably concerned about making it worse.

She drew back and stared at him. "Is it on my face?"

He cupped her chin in his hands and kissed the tip of her nose. "You're as pretty as ever," he said.

She sniffed.

He got her the medication, then served her soup and water. By the time she'd gotten the food down, the itching had subsided. She wanted to stay awake and talk, but she was exhausted. Her eyes drifted closed. The last thing she remembered was Craig sitting on the bed, stroking the back of her hand. She fell asleep to the thought that Krystal Haynes had been the stupidest woman on the face of the planet.

It was light the next time she woke up. Instead of Craig sitting in the chair by her bed, she saw a familiar dark-haired brunette with laughing brown eyes and an impish smile.

"Kim?"

"Hey, you're alive," her friend said and leaned forward in the chair. "How are you feeling?"

"Everything hurts and itches." She shifted uncomfortably. "What are you doing here?"

"I called yesterday to say hi, and Craig told me what had happened. I volunteered to come look after you." Kim's smile faded. "Jeez, I feel so bad. I can't believe you got the chicken pox."

"Don't remind me."

"This is all my fault."

Was it just her imagination, or was everyone in her life suddenly willing to take the blame for her misfortunes? "It's nobody's fault. It just happened."

"But if I hadn't run off with Brian—"

"You wouldn't be happily married now." She reached for the glass of water on the nightstand, but it was just out of reach. Kim grabbed it and handed it to her, hovering near the bed in case Jill couldn't hold it herself.

"Thanks," Jill said, and took a sip. The cool water eased the dryness in her throat. She still felt hot and slightly out of focus. "Do I have a fever?"

"Last time I checked, it was around a hundred. It's come down a little, so we think you'll live."

"Oh, thanks." She raised the glass and held it against her forehead. "How is everyone holding up?"

"Fine. These boys are a handful. How do you manage?"

"It's not so bad."

Kim settled in the chair. She pulled her legs up close to her chest and wrapped her arms around her calves. Her blue-black hair gleamed in the sunlight filtering through the curtains.

"That's easy for you to say," Kim told her. "Every fifteen minutes at least one of them asks if you're going to be okay. The youngest—" She hesitated, as if trying to remember his name.

"Danny."

"Yeah, Danny. He thinks it's his fault because he got sick first."

"I hope you told him it wasn't."

"Of course. But I think he needs to hear it from you. Maybe you could tell him when he gets home from school."

"Hmm, I will." Her eyelids felt heavy. She set the glass on the nightstand.

Kim stood up. "I better get some soup into you before you fall asleep again." She walked to the door, then turned back. "I owe you big-time, Jill."

"Just be happy with Brian."

"I am."

"And name your firstborn after me."

Kim laughed. "Even if it's a boy?"

"Especially if it's a boy."

* * *

Five days later Jill was so bored she wanted to scream. The rash was gone, as was Kim. She'd convinced Danny that her getting sick wasn't his fault. They'd had a long discussion about germs, and now he wanted to be a doctor so he could kill them all. Kim had returned to her new husband and job, the boys were in school and Craig was at the station. The only reason Jill was still in bed was that she'd promised to stay in her room for one more day.

"But I'm bored!" she said loudly. There was no one to hear her complaint, although she felt better voicing it out loud.

Craig had brought in a portable television and set it up on the dresser. It didn't help. She didn't know enough about the story lines on the soaps to be interested and talk shows made her squirm. How could those people confess all those personal things in public?

She tried reading, but she was too restless. She'd been stuck in bed for a week. Her muscles had probably atrophied to the consistency of taffy. The only saving grace was that she hadn't been very interested in food, so she'd lost a couple of pounds.

She glanced around the room, searching for something to do. Her gaze settled on the open bathroom door. She would kill for a shower. She threw back the covers and rose to her feet. The room circled around once before settling in one place. As she walked slowly toward the bathroom, she consoled herself with the thought that she wasn't actually breaking her word. She was still staying in her room. Sort of.

She glanced in the mirror and grimaced. Her hair was matted, her face pale. Her eyes were huge and dark. She looked like a refugee from a war zone.

She splashed water on her face, then brushed her teeth. After turning on the shower, she pulled off her nightshirt and tossed it in the dirty clothes hamper. Her underwear followed. Then she stepped into the steamy spray.

The warm water was heaven. She washed her hair twice, then used a deep conditioner. Although the activity drained her, she didn't leave the stall. It felt too good to be up and moving around. Besides, when she felt shaky, she simply leaned against the tile walls.

After ten minutes, she gave her hair a final rinse and quickly washed the rest of her. She was weak but focused. Thank goodness the fever was gone. She hated that half-here, half-somewhere-else feeling.

She pushed open the glass door and stepped onto the floor mat. As she reached for her towel, her fingers brushed against the bare towel rack. She'd forgotten to put one out.

Suddenly the bathroom door flew open, and Craig stepped inside.

"What the hell are you doing?" he asked, his tone furious. He took in her appearance, turned quickly and opened the cabinet above the toilet. Not looking at her, he grabbed a towel and thrust it toward her. So much for dazzling him with her naked self.

She clutched the towel loosely around herself. He was in uniform. As always, he took her breath away. Of course, in her weakened condition, that was easier than usual. His brows pulled together in a frown, giving him the appearance of an angry deity. He radiated strength and male passion. Desire made her tremble.

The weakness in her knees wasn't all from her illness. She wanted him.

"Well?" he demanded, reminding her he'd asked what she'd been doing.

Wasn't it obvious? "Taking a shower."

"Damn it, Jill, I came home to check on you, and you weren't in bed. I called and called, and you didn't answer." He still wasn't looking at her. Okay, she was a little weak and pale, but she wasn't hideous-looking, was she?

"I was in the shower. I couldn't hear you." She was dripping and starting to feel a little cold. Not to mention a little naked. If only she could get him to notice. She eyed the bathroom floor, trying to figure out exactly how long it was. Would he fit there? It might be uncomfortable, but she was starting not to mind the thought. She giggled softly. Insane thoughts. Maybe the fever wasn't all gone. Maybe it had burned away her second thoughts.

"You promised not to get out of bed."

"No, I promised not to leave my room. Technically, this is still part of my room."

He swore under his breath, then just stood there, not looking at her. Almost as if he didn't notice that she was naked. But she noticed. Water dripped from her hair and cooled her skin, while her lascivious thoughts heated it. The combination made her break out in tiny goose bumps. Her breasts strained toward him. She knew that if she looked down, her nipples would be hard. When the hell was he going to notice she was wearing nothing but a towel?

"I'm really sorry, Craig. I didn't mean to worry you. I just wanted to take a shower." She gave up. He *wasn't* going to notice. "If you're done yelling at me, could you please leave so I can get dressed?"

As soon as she said the words, he sucked in a breath. His gaze raked her body. She felt it as strongly as a touch, as if he'd slipped his hands from her breasts down her belly to the apex of her thighs. Desire filled her, making her most feminine place swell and dampen. She moistened her lips in anticipation of his kiss.

Without saying a word, he turned on his heel and left the room.

"Are you even going to say goodbye?" she asked softly, as the door slammed behind him. Her cheeks burned as if he'd slapped her. In a way he had.

There she was, seminaked before him, and he hadn't even bothered with a come-on. She buried her face in the towel, then raised her head and glanced at the mirror.

Her moan was involuntary. Her wet hair hung down. Water collected on the pointy ends and dripped steadily. Her nose was red, her eyes wide. She looked like a drowned kitten. No wonder he hadn't wanted her.

"I should be h-happy," she said, her voice cracking on the last word. But she wasn't. He didn't want her. Aaron hadn't wanted her. No one wanted her.

She knew she was behaving irrationally. It was just her weakened condition. That didn't stop the tears from spilling onto her cheeks, or a sob from breaking free.

Craig must have been waiting for her right outside the door because he was at her side in an instant.

"Jill? What's wrong?"

"N-nothing," she said. "N-nothing at a-all. I look like a drowned k-kitten. No one wants me."

He made comforting noises deep in his throat as he wrapped the towel securely around her. She wanted to tell him not to treat her like a child, but she liked the way she felt when he lifted her up in his arms.

He sat on the edge of the bed and settled her on his lap. "I want you," he said.

She sniffed loudly and brushed her wet hair off her forehead. "No you don't. You're just saying that to be polite."

His dark gaze met hers. "I'm not that nice."

He'd wrapped the towel around her tightly, but she was sitting on the corner. When she shifted, it loosened. It started to slip down, but she didn't do anything to stop it. Instead, she placed her hands on his shoulders.

"Are you sure?" she asked.

He pulled her closer. She felt the hardness of his arousal press against her hip. "Very sure." He reached up and grabbed her wrists, lifting her hands away. "Jill, you're the one who keeps putting the brakes on a personal relationship. Are you saying you've changed your mind?"

"I—" She didn't have an answer to that. Nothing made sense. She studied his face, his familiar features. She trusted him. She liked him. She wanted him. Maybe it was a reaction to being sick. She didn't know. "I'm just so tired of being alone," she said.

He nodded slowly. "Me, too." He put her hands back on his shoulders and wrapped his arms around her. Then his mouth found hers and she didn't feel alone anymore.

## Chapter Eleven

She responded instantly. When Craig tightened his arms around her, she drew him into her mouth, as if she were starving and he her only hope of survival.

He angled his head, dipping his tongue inside, tasting her sweetness mingling with the mint of toothpaste. She smelled fresh and clean, her body was warm. He wanted to strip her towel off her and take her right there, that minute. The need inside him had flared to life with a painful intensity that sucked the air from his lungs. But instead of giving in, he hung on, because he needed this to be magic for her. His pleasure depended as much on chasing her to paradise and making her lose control as it did on finding a place of refuge between her silky thighs.

So instead of tilting her back and burying himself inside her, he kept his hands on her arms. He had to get control before he risked touching her anywhere else.

He brushed his tongue over hers, circling her, discovering the sweet secrets of her mouth. His lips pressed harder, demanding more, and she gave all she had to him. She leaned toward him, arching her body against him. Her towel slipped lower. He sensed it, more than felt it. When he could bear it no longer, he raised his head and looked at her.

The soft yellow terry cloth pooled at her waist, exposing her torso. Her hair was still damp and rumpled, her face pale, her eyes wide and unfocused. She smiled at him, a "come love me" kind of smile that upped the pressure in his groin about fifty percent.

He could see her collarbone, the faint dusting of freckles on her creamy skin. His gaze dipped lower to her breasts. His breath caught in his throat. Without conscious thought, he raised his hands and cupped her perfect round flesh.

She was large for her petite frame and the lush curves filled his palms. She responded instantly to his embrace, moaning his name and leaning forward to press a kiss to his throat. Her hot breath and warm lips taunted him, as did the feel of her in his hands.

She was warm, living satin. Supple, soft, sensual. He traced her curves, then ran his thumbs over the taut points of her coral-tipped nipples. A ripple shot through her and she exhaled his name.

With one easy movement, he kicked off his shoes, then stretched out on the bed. She tumbled next to him. He caught her, cushioning her fall. The fluffy towel tangled around her. He left it in place, liking the peek-aboo effect. He saw one breast, a bit of her right thigh, her belly and the lower part of her legs. One arm was trapped by the terry cloth.

He turned and supported himself on one elbow. With his free hand, he touched her face.

"You're so beautiful," he murmured.

She smiled. "Hardly."

"You are. Your eyes were the first thing I noticed about you."

She wrinkled her nose. "I look like a kitten. It's not a comparison most people aspire to."

"I saw the likeness at first," he admitted, "but now I just see you."

He stroked her cheek, then her nose. He followed the path down to her mouth. She parted her lips. Her tongue darted out and licked the tip of his finger. Instantly fire shot through him.

He swore under his breath.

She smiled. "Did you like that?"

"Let's just say I'd like anything you did right now." He circled her mouth with his finger.

She leaned her head forward, opened her mouth and captured his finger. She drew him in deeply, then suckled him, circling his sensitized skin with her tongue.

The movement mimicked what they would do later, the completion of their act of love. It was as if someone had hooked up a direct circuit from his index finger to his groin. Sensation raced down, engorging him, making him flex painfully against the fly of his trousers. His skin heated to the point of burning.

He pulled his finger free and kissed her. Passion caught him in its grip until he feared for his control. In the back of his mind was the constant worry that she was so small. He didn't want to hurt her.

He plunged his tongue inside, as if daring her to do with that what she'd done with his finger. She obliged him until he thought he might explode. He retreated and she followed. While she touched and tasted his mouth, he clamped his lips around her and tormented her in return. She writhed beneath him.

He stroked her bare arm, then her midriff. Brushing the towel aside, he cupped the curve of her hip, then traced her thighs. She was all woman, all curves, in a compact package. He reversed his steps until he cupped her breast. While his fingers teased her already tight nipple, he broke the kiss and trailed down her throat. She arched her head back, urging him on.

He tasted her skin and explored her smooth chest, before dipping lower. A quick jerk freed her of the towel. He tossed it over his shoulder and she was bare to his gaze.

He stared at her full breasts, then at her narrow waist and the sweep of her hips. At the apex of her thighs, her curls were only a shade or two darker than the hair on her head. He placed his hand on her belly. His little finger nestled in her curls, his thumb nearly touched her breasts. She was too small.

If he'd been any kind of gentleman, he would have stopped. Instead, his mind raced to find a dozen different ways to make it work. It had to be possible. If he didn't make love with her, he would die.

He tried to remember how long it had been since he'd touched a woman intimately. Months. Years. He'd begun to think he would never experience that particular pleasure again. After a while, his body had ceased wanting the release and he'd put that part of his life on hold. He'd always equated lovemaking with love, having given up mindless sex shortly after his teens. He didn't love Jill—at least he assumed he didn't. But this intimacy felt right. Maybe it was what she'd said. They were both tired of being alone. He trusted her. That was more than what he could have said about Krystal.

"What are you thinking?" she asked, reaching for the first button on his uniform shirt.

"That I'm going to hurt you. You're too small."

She laughed and her breasts bounced in time with her amusement. He wanted to beg her to do it again, but his mouth was dry and he couldn't speak. He lowered his head and took one of her nipples in his mouth.

She grabbed his head as if to hold him in place. He wanted to tell her he had no plans to go anywhere, but that would have meant stopping. Instead, he rolled the tight point between his lips. He circled her with his tongue, then lifted his mouth slightly and blew on the damp flesh.

Her hips tilted toward him, her grip on his hair tightened. He moved to her other breast and repeated his ministrations. Her arms fell to her sides as she rocked her head from side to side. With each breath, she moaned.

He placed his hand flat on her belly, then slid it lower until his fingers encountered her curls. He could feel the softness of her, the dampness. Lower and lower until her waiting warmth enveloped him. The temptation of slick heat was more than he could resist. He eased one finger inside of her.

Instantly, she parted her thighs. He tested the tight circle that would milk him to ecstasy. Her muscles clenched around him and he groaned.

Even as his tongue traced a tight circle over her nipple, his fingers found a matching taut peak between her legs. He circled that place, too, moving around and around before stroking over it. Once. Quickly.

Her hips flexed toward him. Her breathing rate increased, as did the temperature of her skin. He brushed the spot, inciting the same response. As he drew his head down her body, pausing to lick her belly and nip at her side, he moved his fingers rhythmically. He picked up speed to match her breathing. She clawed at the sheets and called his name. He nibbled on her hipbone, then traced a line through her curls and finally bent low so he could replace his hand with his mouth.

At the first touch of his tongue, she screamed, though it wasn't especially loud. The sound had a half-embarrassed quality to it that made him smile.

His body was doing some screaming of its own. The fire between his legs had reached the point of being unbearable, but he didn't stop what he was doing. He'd always enjoyed touching a woman everywhere, tasting her, bringing her to pleasure first. If he waited until they climaxed together, he didn't get to watch her, or listen to her breathing, or see the flush on her skin. It took away from the experience. So even as his erection throbbed and flexed, and his muscles tightened in anticipation, he slowed the cadence of his tongue against her most feminine place.

He circled her, sweeping around, but not touching the vibrating place of need. He dipped inside her, then returned to the tiny place. Only when her breath came in pants and her bent legs trembled did he move faster, bringing her quickly to the point of release.

She hung there for a heartbeat, her body unbelievably tight. He flicked his tongue quickly, then slipped a finger inside her and pressed upward, as if to caress the spot from both sides.

She convulsed around him. She trembled and shook. Powerful contractions squeezed his finger as he felt and watched her experience perfection. As he continued to touch her gently, lightly, she rode the crest of fulfillment until at last it slowed and she was still.

He sat up and stared at her. Her irises were huge. A flush covered her chest. She blinked several times as if the world was just now coming into focus.

"I think the earth moved," she said, her voice sounding stunned.

He smiled.

"I'm not kidding. I think I've been doing it wrong all these years. It's never been—" She exhaled. "You should teach a class. Trust me, you could make a fortune."

He bent over and kissed her. She locked her arms around him, holding him close.

"Thank you," she whispered.

"You're welco—"

She slipped her tongue into his ear. Instantly, his body stiffened. Delicious tingles raced through him. She nipped his lobe, then moved lower and sucked on his neck. Her teeth grated erotically.

He braced his weight on his arms, determined to let her have her way with him. She reached for the buttons on his shirt and began unfastening them. By the time she'd pulled the cloth free from his trousers, he'd begun to shake.

She raised herself up slightly and, as she drew the shirt apart, placed her mouth against his chest. She trailed kisses from his throat to his waistband. She circled her tongue through the hair until she found his nipples, then teased him into mindlessness.

When he couldn't stand it anymore, he pushed himself into a sitting position and ripped off his shirt. She sat up, completely naked and apparently unselfconscious.

Her hands followed the path the shirt had taken. She touched his shoulders, then stroked down his arms. She knelt before him, her breasts swaying free. He reached for them, cupping her gently. She tilted her head back.

"I can't believe how that makes me feel," she said.

"It does a lot for me, too." His voice was hoarse.

Keeping her head back, she leaned toward him so that her breasts brushed against his chest. The faint touch of her taut nipples was a pleasing form of torture. She swayed back and forth, keeping her balance by resting her hands on his shoulders. Suddenly she stopped and stared at him. Her green eyes widened.

"Oh, Craig, I'm not on the Pill anymore."

Birth control. Protection. He should have thought of it before. He grinned. Who'd had the time?

"I've got some condoms upstairs," he said, sliding off the bed.

She stood up and shook her head. "You stay right here. I'll get them. Where are they?"

"My nightstand. On the left side, top drawer."

She started out of the room, then glanced over her shoulder at him. "While I'm gone, feel free to take off the rest of your clothes."

He watched her leave, then did as she requested, quickly pulling off his socks, then stepping out of his trousers and briefs. Once that was done, he didn't know whether he should sit on the side of the bed or lie down.

He glanced at himself and frowned. His arousal was so *obvious*. He didn't want to scare her off. He was still worried about the size problem. His finger had slipped inside her easily enough, but this was a little . . . larger.

Before he could figure out what to do, she'd returned with a small box of condoms. She touched the top. "Unopened."

"I just bought them."

She moved to the side of the bed. "I'm glad."

He'd settled on a sitting position. When she stepped in front of him, he was glad. He took the box from her and set it on the nightstand, then grabbed her hips and lifted her onto his lap. She straddled him, his arousal trapped between their bellies. She wiggled and he almost lost his control right there.

"Damn it, woman!" he growled.

She giggled. "I love it when you talk dirty."

He stared at her. "Are you feeling all right?"

"Fishing for more compliments?"

"No. You just spent a week in bed. I don't want to overdo it."

"I'm a little tired, but I think I can stay awake for another five or ten minutes."

"It'll take longer than that," he said.

She smiled. "Not if I do my job right."

He raised his hand and touched her cheek. "I didn't think you'd be like this."

"Like what?"

"So comfortable with yourself and me. You don't mind being naked."

She surprised him by blushing. "I'm not normally like this. You make me feel comfortable." She shrugged. "Maybe comfortable isn't the right word. I can see that you want me. The way you watch me makes me feel very attractive and feminine."

"You are."

"Shut up and kiss me."

He obliged her. He tilted his head and pressed his mouth against her. She opened for him immediately and took him with a passion that sent his control into the next dimension. Suddenly he had to touch her everywhere, be with her, in her. Damn it, she was already wet and naked. What more did he want?

He touched her back, her thighs, her breasts, then fumbled for the box of protection. Even as he was sliding back on the bed, he ripped the box open and pulled out a condom. He was shaking so badly he could barely open the package.

Once he was stretched out on the mattress, she rained kisses on his chest.

"You're not helping," he said, trying to smooth the latex sheath over himself.

She wiggled against his thighs and licked a damp circle around his belly button. "I'm not trying to."

At last it was in place. He looked at her. "I want you on top. You'll have more control."

She nodded, then raised herself up on her knees. He reached his hand between them and placed the other on her hip. Inch by inch, she lowered herself on him.

He watched her face, trying to judge if he was hurting her. She closed her eyes and smiled. If her look of pleasure was anything to go by, he fit just fine. He let go of his worries as he guided her down. Every part of him focused on the damp heat surrounding him. Her body stretched to accommodate him, sliding slowly, caressing him like a benediction.

When she would have rocked her hips, he stilled her with his hands. "Not yet," he groaned, between clenched teeth.

"I told you it wouldn't take but five minutes," she murmured, her tone teasing.

He told himself it was because it had been so long, but he knew it was also about Jill. As his gaze focused on her face, then dropped lower to her breasts, he knew it was specifically about her.

The thought should have scared him to death, but strangely, it didn't.

He released his hold on her hips and she began to move. He helped her find the rhythm. As they rocked together, her body continued to stretch around him, allowing him to go deeper. He arched up, filling her until she took all of him.

"Do it," she said.

Her permission was all he needed. His mind cleared of everything but the need for release. He thrust against her quickly, moving up and down. She matched his movements, adding friction that would send him over the edge.

He tried to focus on her, on her head tilted back, on the sleek, pure lines of her neck, on the way her breasts swayed and bounced, on her hands splaying and releasing. He could feel her muscles tightening as she took pleasure in their joining. The pressure built inside him. He wouldn't be able to hold back.

He reached his hand between them, then slipped his thumb into her damp curls. He touched her most sensitive spot and pressed, allowing her to find the rhythm that would please her most. She caught her breath. He pressed harder. Instantly her body began to ripple and clench. It was all he needed. The world disappeared into a rush of pleasure so intense he lost contact with everything but the feel of her body around him and the sound of his name on her lips.

When he finally focused again, Jill sagged against him in contentment. "I could die a happy person right now," she said.

"I know what you mean."

She snuggled against him like the kitten she compared herself to. "Hmm, I can hear the vibration of your voice through your chest. Say something again."

He stroked her short hair. "What do you want me to say?"

There was no answer. He raised his head. Jill was stretched out on his chest, her eyes closed, her breathing even. Exhaustion had caught up with her.

He half rose into a sitting position so he could snag the covers. She didn't stir. He pulled the sheet and light blanket over both of them, then glanced at the clock. They had a couple of hours until the boys had to be picked up at school. He wrapped his arms around her and listened to her heart beating in time with his.

When she awoke it was night. Jill blinked in the darkness. She distinctly remembered it being daylight when she'd last been awake. She'd taken a shower and then—

She froze, terrified of the memories crashing in on her. She'd behaved like a wanton, throwing herself at Craig. Oh, Lord, what must he think of her?

She lay very still, trying to figure out if she was alone or not. This bedroom was at the back of the house, so there wasn't any streetlight filtering through the drapes to help. She listened for breathing, but didn't hear any but her own. Finally she shifted to see the clock and bumped into something very warm and very naked in her bed. She winced.

"It's nearly midnight," he said.

"Oh, my. How long have I been asleep?"

"About eight hours. I guess I tired you out."

She didn't have to see him to know he was smiling. She could hear it in his voice. A blush flared on her cheeks. "Oh, Craig, I'm sorry."

He reached for her and pulled her against him. Arms and legs tangled together until he settled back with her head on his shoulder and his arms around her.

"What are you sorry about?" he asked.

"I—" She could lie and say she was sorry for falling asleep like that, but somehow she didn't think he would buy it.

"Are you feeling okay?" he asked.

"Yes. I feel great. Renewed, in fact." She drew in a deep breath and let it out slowly. "I didn't mean to do that."

"Make love?"

She nodded, rubbing her cheek against his bare skin. "I threw myself at you. I don't even want to think about it."

He chuckled. "I do. In fact, I can't seem to think about anything else."

She buried her face in his side and moaned. "I can't believe I used you the same way everyone has used me. Just to get what I wanted. I'm slime. I'm lower than slime. I'm silt sludge that aspires to be slime."

He drew away from her for a second and clicked on the bedside light. Then he fluffed up the pillows and pushed them behind him so he was sitting up.

"Number one," he said, looking at her. "No one did anything they didn't want to do, least of all me. I'm glad we made love, Jill, and I'd like it better if you didn't have any regrets, either."

"But, I—"

"No. You didn't. You didn't throw yourself at me or coerce me. I haven't been with a woman in a long time. I thought that part of me was dead. I'm glad to know it's not."

"But—"

He smiled. "You worry too much. Can't you just be happy it felt so good?"

"But isn't it going to be awkward now? What will we say to each other? How will we act in front of the boys? Doesn't this change everything?"

"No."

She waited but he didn't say anything else. "That's it? Just 'no'?"

He winked.

"Damn it, Craig."

Without warning, he slipped down the mattress and grabbed her, hauling her close. "I love it when you talk dirty," he said.

She wanted to resist. She wanted to have a rational conversation. They couldn't just ignore what had happened. Then his fingers trailed across her breasts and she thought that maybe they could.

"I don't want to hurt you if you're sore," he murmured against her breast.

"I'm fine." She ran her fingers across his chest, savoring the contrast of cool hair and warm skin. She lingered over his heart and felt the rapid pounding.

"You're sure?"

She reached her hand down and touched his arousal. As she'd hoped, that shut him up.

They moved together in a dance of desire, taking what they'd already learned about each other and applying it to make the sensations more intense, the pleasure more incredible. When he moved to shift her on top of him, she shook her head.

"I want you on top," she said.

"I'm afraid I'll hurt you."

"I'll be fine," she said. "I trust you."

As he knelt between her thighs and slowly entered her, she wondered how long it had been since she'd trusted anyone, let alone a man. Then he withdrew, only to thrust inside her again, and the question was forgotten in the magic of the moment.

Craig was gone when she woke up. She vaguely remembered a quick goodbye kiss before he left for the station. She rolled over and stared at the clock. It was going to ring in ten minutes, then she would go wake up the boys. Ben was probably already up. He'd told her that he was walking without her. She was proud of him. He'd lost most of the weight and he looked terrific.

She sat up and turned off the alarm, then reached for her robe. Before she could stagger into the bathroom, the phone rang. She had an extension in her room. She reached for it, smiling in anticipation, knowing Craig had called to say good-morning.

"Hello?" she said.

"Hi, uh, it's Jill, right?" The unfamiliar voice sounded panicked.

"Yes, this is Jill Bradford."

"Great. I'm Kyle. Craig's youngest brother. Is he there?"

"No, he's left for the station."

"Oh, God. Okay. Damn. Um, could you tell him—" Kyle drew in an audible breath. "Oh, God. It's Sandy. She's having the baby. Now. Soon. We're leaving for the hospital now and if you could tell him.'' He swore again. ''She's had three, so this is no big deal for her, but I don't think I can go through this. Anyway, tell Craig to hurry.''

He hung up without saying goodbye.

She stared at the phone for a moment, then dialed the station. She was put through to Craig immediately.

''I already know,'' he said. ''Travis called. Look, I don't want to take the boys out of school. They missed too many days being sick. Pack enough for everyone for the weekend, then after you pick them up, swing by the station and get me. I'm glad we've nearly wrapped up that case with the elderly drivers so I can take the weekend off.''

''Weekend off? I'm confused. What's going on?''

He chuckled. ''Sorry, Jill. This is all new to you, isn't it? Sandy's having her baby. We all have to be there. It's a Haynes brothers tradition. We're *always* there for each other.''

''Which means?''

''We're going to Glenwood.''

## Chapter Twelve

Tiny babies slept on, unaware of the fuss being made over them by the group of people staring at them from the other side of the glass. Craig had done this three times with Krystal, and also with Travis and Austin. He supposed he should be jaded by now, but he wasn't. The sight of the infants' innocent, scrunched-up faces always got him right in the center of his chest.

Jill pointed to one baby in a little pink stocking cap. "That's her."

He stared, amazed. "It must be true."

"What?"

"The Haynes family curse is really broken. After four generations of only boys, Kyle just had the second girl."

Jill frowned, as if in thought. "Now who had the first one?"

"Travis."

"Okay, Travis is married to Sandy?"

He smiled and dropped his arm over her shoulder. "No. Travis is married to Elizabeth."

"I'll never get this straight."

He led her to a bench on the other side of the wide corridor. This might be a hospital, but close to the nursery it didn't feel too antiseptic. When they were seated, he shifted so he was facing her.

"It's very simple," he said.

"For you. I'm an only child, and I'm not even married. Keeping track of my family is a snap."

The color had returned to Jill's face after her illness. She still tired easily—she'd slept the whole way in the car—but the fever was gone and she claimed to have most of her energy back. She wore a simple shirt tucked into black jeans. The shirt was the exact color of her eyes. Makeup emphasized their shape. Her mouth was kissably pink. Delicate gold earrings glittered in the overhead lights.

She was beautiful, and not just because of how she looked. They hadn't had a moment to talk about what had happened yesterday and last night. They'd become lovers, then their world had been turned upside down by the birth of Kyle's daughter. Most women would have been clinging, or whining, wanting to know where things stood. Not that he had an answer for that. They'd gone from friendly to intimate without much in the way of a warning. For all he knew, Jill would want to back off for a while to catch her breath. He didn't know what he wanted, yet. There hadn't been time to think. Whatever their decision, Jill wasn't pressuring him right now and he was grateful.

Their lovemaking had been more than he'd imagined, and he'd imagined a lot. But the thought of committing to anyone, even her, gave him a bad feeling in the pit of his stomach. The risk was too great. He only wanted a sure thing. Even Jill couldn't guarantee that.

While they couldn't talk about themselves in this public setting, he could explain the intricacies of his family.

"I'm one of four brothers," he said. "I'm the oldest. I have three boys."

She smiled. "That part I knew."

"Next comes Travis. He's the sheriff here in Glenwood. He's married to Elizabeth. They have two children, both girls. The oldest, Mandy, is Elizabeth's by a previous marriage."

Jill nodded. "Travis and Elizabeth, two girls. Got it."

"Next is Jordan. He's the black sheep of the family. A fire fighter instead of a cop. He's not married."

"Thank goodness! Less for me to keep track of."

"Then Kyle. He's the youngest and a deputy here in Glenwood. He married Sandy, who had three children from a previous marriage. Two girls, one boy. She's the one who just had the baby. Finally, our friend Austin is married to Rebecca. They adopted a boy and had a boy together. He owns the company we all invested in." He leaned back. "See, very simple."

She stared at him for a moment and then started laughing. "Oh, yeah. Really simple. Why did I ever think it was a problem?"

"Once you meet everyone, you'll be able to put faces with the names."

She shook her head. "Now I know why that house looked like a day-care center when we dropped off the boys."

"Between us, we do have a lot of kids." He started to say more, then heard someone call his name. He glanced up and saw his brothers approaching. Austin was with them.

Craig rose to his feet. Kyle reached him first and gave him a hug that about cracked his ribs. Travis and Jordan joined the pair and added their strength to the embrace. Soon all four brothers were slapping each other on the back. As always, Austin hung just a little outside the circle. Kyle and Jordan parted for him and he stepped inside.

"Who's the redhead?" Jordan asked.

"Who wants to know?" Craig countered, grinning with pride.

The men laughed and separated. Craig held out his hand to Jill. She accepted it and rose slowly to her feet. Her mouth was hanging open slightly. She closed it, looking a little shell-shocked.

"These are my brothers," he said proudly. "And this is Jill. She's the boys' nanny."

Travis and Jordan glanced significantly at his and Jill's clasped hands, then at each other. Eyebrows rose. He knew what they were thinking. Let 'em, he told himself. Maybe he would get lucky and it would be true.

He moved behind Jill and placed his hands on her shoulders. "Starting from left to right. Kyle, Austin, Jordan and Travis."

She shook hands with each of them in turn. "I'm never going to keep you straight."

"It's easy," Kyle told her. "I'm the best looking and the smartest. Austin's wearing an earring. Travis is maybe an inch taller than me, and Jordan doesn't talk much."

Travis leaned behind the other two men and cuffed Kyle. "I'm better looking."

"I'm smarter," Jordan said.

"I won't argue with the earring," Austin said.

"Oh, my." Jill sounded uncertain.

"You okay?" Craig asked.

"It's a little overwhelming." She craned her neck. "You didn't tell me everyone was so tall. This is some gene pool."

Austin looked down at her. "The Haynes brothers are short, but we put up with them."

"Short?" Jill laughed. "Maybe to you and your friends." She rotated her shoulders. "My neck already hurts from looking up."

Travis elbowed his way between Craig and Jill. "Don't monopolize the lady, brother." Travis took Jill's arm and led her down the corridor. "I'm sure my brother hasn't told you everything about the family. There are a couple of things I'd like to clarify and maybe one or two stories you'd like to hear."

Jill gave Craig a helpless look over her shoulder, but Travis insisted.

"You'll be fine," Craig told her, watching them go. He wasn't concerned. Travis might tease him, but he would never do anything mean-spirited. He turned his attention to the youngest of the Haynes brothers. "How are you feeling?"

Kyle shrugged. "I keep telling myself Sandy did all the hard work, but jeez, Craig, I'm still shaking."

Craig patted his brother on the back. "It gets worse for a while, but then it gets better. At least Sandy's had babies in the house. She'll know what to do."

"What if—" Kyle cleared his throat. "What if I'm not a good father?"

Craig glanced at him, then at Jordan. They all had the famous Haynes good looks. Dark hair and eyes, muscular bodies. They were intelligent, funny and caring. And they were all scared to death of screwing up the way their father had.

Travis had been through a divorce before he found Elizabeth. Before falling for Sandy, Kyle had made a practice of dumping women before they could dump him. Jordan seemed to go through his life avoiding emotional commitments of any kind, and no one knew why. He, Craig, had married Krystal. Enough said.

"You can do your best," he told his brother. "That's the only advice I can give you. Every day, try to do your best. Anyway, you already know how to be a dad. You're father to Sandy's three kids."

Kyle hunched his shoulders. Like Jordan and Austin, he was wearing jeans and a shirt. Only Craig and Travis were in uniform. "This is different. Sandy's kids were already grown-up enough to have personalities. I didn't think there was much I could do wrong. But this is a baby."

"A girl," Craig said. "Two miracles."

"The curse is broken," Jordan said.

Craig didn't want to think about that. "Speaking of Sandy's kids, Jill and I can take them for a few days if you'd like. We talked about it on the way down."

"Thanks." Kyle punched him in the arm. "Austin and Rebecca have already offered. They've got the most room, and we won't have to take anyone out of school. It'll be easier staying local."

"They want to stay with us because of the upstairs playroom," Austin said.

"No problem," Craig said. "Just thought I'd offer."

Kyle nodded. "I appreciate it. Everyone is pitching in. That's one of the things I like best about this family. Even Louise is going to come stay with Sandy and me for the first month."

"She's a big help," Craig said. At the mention of Louise, Jordan got the oddest look on his face. Anger and something else. Betrayal maybe? From Louise? That didn't make sense. The older woman had been working for Travis for several years. Since the brothers had started marrying and having children, she'd been helping out. Everyone liked her.

Kyle stared at the tight circle of friends. "You guys ever think it would turn out like this?"

"No," Craig said easily. "I didn't think we'd get this lucky." He was talking about them all staying friends, but Kyle meant something else.

"I never thought I would be this happy," he said, then shrugged. "I know that sounds lame."

"No, it doesn't," Jordan said. "Not after what we went through."

"I never thought I'd get this lucky," Austin said quietly.

Craig remembered his friend's past. Austin had been abandoned by his mother when he was just a kid. It was during his time at the Glenwood orphanage that he'd met and made friends with the Haynes brothers. He'd grown from a skinny, hostile kid into a successful entrepreneur. After years of holding himself apart, he'd finally found his way into a circle of love. All because of a woman named Rebecca and her unwillingness to give up on the man she loved.

Thinking about the past kept Craig from dealing with the present. He had to fight down feelings of envy as he stared at his brothers and Austin. They'd found something wonderful with someone special. They'd found love.

He glanced at Jordan and saw the same conflicting emotions reflected in his brother's gaze. What had the two of them done wrong? Krystal had been mistake number one for him. What was the name of Jordan's mistake?

Damn it, nothing was easy. He wanted what Travis, Kyle and Austin had. He wanted to believe in someone again, but it was hard. Krystal had scarred him and he wasn't sure he would ever recover. What about Jill? Was he already involved with her and just fooling himself that he wasn't? She was so different from his ex-wife. His feelings were different, too. There was less lightning and a lot more caring.

Krystal had been very high maintenance, but Jill was more concerned about taking care of others. That made him want to take care of her. He admired her, appreciated the way she looked after the boys. She was a dynamo in bed and just thinking about it made his body throb. Was that . . . love?

Even as he asked the question, a voice in his head reminded him that he wasn't going to do this again. Not unless there were guarantees. Besides, more than once Jill had made it clear that she wasn't interested in anything permanent. When her time was up, she would be gone.

The huge table sat twenty, and nearly every chair had been used. Jill stood up with the other two women and helped clear the table. The men made a halfhearted attempt to offer assistance. Elizabeth brushed them off with a good-natured, "Oh, please, we know you're lying!"

The sound of laughter accompanied Jill into the kitchen. Once there, she paused to admire the spacious room. A huge greenhouse window offered a view of the rolling grass and the forest beyond. At least that's what she'd been told. It had been dusk when they'd arrived at Rebecca and Austin's house.

Bleached cabinets hugged the walls. The tile was white, the appliances black, and the floor was the same bleached wood as the cabinets. Blue-and-white wallpaper added color to the large room.

"Impressive," Jill said softly as she put the dishes down on the counter.

"I like it."

She spun toward the sound and saw Rebecca walking toward her carrying an armful of plates and silverware. Austin's wife was taller than Jill, but most people were. She had long, curly dark hair and the kind of face that would make a perfect cameo. She wore a flowing dress that stopped midway between her knees and ankles, and Jill had the impression that Rebecca Lucas belonged in a gentler time. She wondered what this delicate-looking woman was doing with a husband who looked like a dark pirate and even had the earring.

Rebecca approached and put down the plates. "I'm sure you're still feeling overwhelmed."

"A little."

"You'll get used to everyone. I had the advantage of getting to know Travis first, then his brothers. By the time Austin and I—" She paused and a faint blush stained her cheeks.

"Dated?" Jill offered helpfully.

The blush deepened. "Austin and I never really dated. We just sort of got married. I had a crush on

him for years, then one night..." She waved her hand.
"It's a long story. I'll tell it to you sometime. Anyway,
I already knew everyone. Elizabeth also met the
brothers a few at a time. And Sandy had known them
from when she lived here in Glenwood and had gone to
school with them. I can't imagine what it must be like
for you, coming in cold like this."

"Sandy's easy," Jill said and grinned. "She's still in
the hospital, so I don't have to worry about her. Everyone else is confusing. It's not just the adults, it's the
kids."

Rebecca tilted her head toward the noise coming
from the living room. "There are a bunch." Rebecca
lifted the cover off a large chocolate cake. "Could you
get the plates, please? We'll need..." She counted on
her fingers. "Kyle left for the hospital so that's seven
adults and ten kids. Is that right?"

Jill laughed. "You're asking the wrong person.
You'd better cut up the whole cake. I'm sure there
won't be leftovers."

"Good idea."

As Rebecca filled the plates, Jill carried them into the
dining room. The children returned to their seats. She
put a piece in front of Ben. He looked at her question-
ingly. She bent close to his ear.

"It's up to you," she murmured. "If you want to eat
it, then go ahead. You're doing great. If you think it's
going to make you feel bad, then don't."

He nodded. "I'll just have half," he said, reaching
for a knife and carefully cutting the cake into two
pieces.

She dropped a quick kiss on the top of his head before returning to the kitchen. By the time everyone had
been served, Elizabeth announced that the coffee was

done. Cups were poured and passed around the table. There was a lull in the conversation. Elizabeth raised her cup.

"I'd like to propose a toast. To the infamous Haynes brothers and their friends."

Jill took a sip of coffee, then leaned toward Craig. "Why are you infamous?"

Austin heard the question. "You haven't told her?" the dark-eyed pirate asked.

Craig groaned. "Don't start on this. It was a long time ago. We've all grown up and matured."

"What was a long time ago?" Jill wanted to know.

Elizabeth leaned forward and grinned. "Honey, the stories we could tell you about these boys. They would make your hair curl."

"Like what?"

"Can I please be excused?" a girl about C.J.'s age asked.

"Me, too," Danny said. "You guys are just gonna talk about the olden days."

Craig looked at Travis, then shrugged. "All children are excused. Go to the playroom and try to get along."

The kids cheered as they raced from the room. Within seconds, footsteps thundered on the stairs as the horde ascended to what Jill supposed was a huge playroom. The Lucas family didn't seem to do anything by halves.

Rebecca glanced at her husband. "The Haynes brothers and Austin turned dating into an art form. From what I understand, there wasn't a girl in a twenty-mile radius who was safe from them."

"Cheerleaders," Elizabeth said. "Brainy types, flirts, shy ones. It didn't matter. No one was immune to their charm."

"Really?" Jill glanced at Craig, who was squirming in his chair. Travis and Jordan didn't look any more comfortable. Even Austin seemed to find the silverware on the table fascinating.

"None of us do that anymore," Craig said.

"I don't understand," Jill said. "You're saying that all the brothers were—"

"Heartbreakers," Rebecca said. "They loved 'em and left 'em. Tempting them with promises, then—"

"I never made promises," Craig said heatedly.

"I was up-front from the beginning," Travis added.

Elizabeth leaned over and kissed her husband on the mouth. For that second, their love was as tangible as the table itself. Jill felt a flicker of envy.

"We know that," Elizabeth said. "We're just teasing you because we love you."

"That's right," Rebecca added. "After all, look at how you've changed."

"Jordan hasn't," Travis said, obviously pleased to have the attention on someone else. "He's holding out and needs a woman."

Jordan shook his head. "Don't forget Craig. He needs a woman, too."

Austin lifted his eyebrows. "Maybe not."

Now it was Jill's turn to blush.

"You didn't answer the question, Jordan," Craig said. "Anyone special in your life?"

"I've sworn off women."

Rebecca laughed. "We'll find you someone." She rose to her feet and began collecting dessert plates. "Didn't we just clear this table?"

"Yes, you did, and now it's our turn." Austin stood and shooed her toward the living room. "You ladies go talk about us while we finish."

"You don't have to ask me twice." Elizabeth linked arms with Rebecca. The two of them came around and collected Jill. Together they walked into the living room.

The huge space had been designed for comfort. There was a rock fireplace in one corner, with three sofas scattered around. A few wing chairs completed the conversation grouping. Tables were bare except for a couple of floral arrangements. Paintings of outdoor scenes, women with children and one seascape hung on the walls. The predominant colors were rose and cream, with colonial blue accents. The effect was that of space and comfort. Children would be welcome here. There was nothing for them to break or ruin. The room would easily seat twenty, yet gave the impression of being welcoming and intimate.

"I'm impressed," Jill said. "Who did the decorating?"

"I did," Rebecca answered. "Austin helped. We preplanned the room on his computer. After that, it was pretty easy. I assume I got lucky because I don't have an artistic bone in my body."

"You can't tell," Jill said.

Elizabeth sat in a wing chair next to a rose-and-cream-striped sofa. Jill sank down onto the couch and Rebecca joined her. She felt them staring at her.

"What do you want to know?" she asked.

Rebecca laughed. "Elizabeth, something is wrong. We used to be subtle."

"I guess we're out of practice. I suppose it's because we haven't had anyone to interrogate in so long.

Not since Kyle started dating Sandy. Craig brought a couple of women around, but they obviously didn't mean anything to him."

Jill wondered if Elizabeth was implying that Craig was interested in her. She didn't know what to say to that. She and Craig were lovers. No, they'd made love. But they hadn't talked about it. In a way, she was glad. She didn't know what she wanted from him. The thought of a relationship terrified her. The situation was too close to what had happened with Aaron. A single father with kids in need of help. She refused to be used again. She reminded herself Craig was nothing like Aaron, and she believed that with all her heart. Yet she'd been wrong before. She wasn't willing to be wrong again.

"I like Craig," she admitted at last. "We're friends. But I'm really there to look after his boys. Nothing else."

"Too bad," Elizabeth said. "He's a great guy. All the brothers are. It's a shame about their family."

"I know a little about what happened with his father," she said.

Elizabeth grimaced. "That man is a bastard. I get so angry when I think about what he did to his sons." She glanced at Jill. "We tease them about their dating habits when they were young, but the truth is they're all wonderful men."

"They seem very close," Jill said.

"They had to be. I can't imagine what it was like for their mother. I don't blame the poor woman. I just wish she'd been stronger. She should have thrown her husband out."

"I agree." Rebecca sighed. "The past tainted them all. Austin lived a different kind of hell when he was growing up. It still affects him."

Jill had to consciously keep her mouth closed. Rebecca looked as innocent as a nun. She couldn't believe the other woman had actually used a bad word.

"I swear, these men are all walking around with wounded souls," Rebecca continued. "They don't want anybody inside, but they desperately need the loving. I just want to hug them all until they're healed."

"If only it were that simple," Elizabeth said. She glanced up at Jill and smiled guiltily. "Sorry. I didn't mean for this to get so serious."

"I understand," Jill said.

Rebecca leaned forward. "Be kind to Craig, Jill. He deserves that. He's one of the good guys."

Before she could continue, the men strolled into the living room. Elizabeth and Rebecca rose to their feet and walked to their husbands. There was that moment of silent communications. Hands touched, eyes met, half smiles were shared. Austin sat in one of the large chairs and pulled Rebecca onto his lap. She went easily, as if they'd performed this ritual a thousand times before. A young boy of maybe eight or nine raced into the room and joined them, squirming for a place on his father's lap.

Jill stared at the three of them. That must be their adopted boy. Both Austin and Rebecca had dark hair, while the child was blond. Elizabeth sat on a sofa. Travis stretched out and rested his head on her lap. Several more children came into the room.

Craig made his way to where Jill was seated. She held her breath as he paused, then released it when he took the place in the middle, leaving the other side for Danny, who climbed up next to him. He put his arm around the boy, then glanced at her and smiled. Their shoulders brushed. She could inhale the scent of him. For that moment, it was enough.

*Be kind to Craig... He's one of the good guys.* Rebecca's advice repeated over and over in her head. She knew he was a good man. She'd been touched by his kindness.

Lazy conversation filled the room, punctuated by laughter. This was a collection of people who enjoyed being together. Even the children participated. Only Jordan sat alone on the fringes of the room.

As she studied him, she realized he was single and didn't have a child. He should be exactly what she was looking for. Yet she didn't feel even a flicker of interest. She didn't want to go talk to him; she wanted to be next to Craig.

Dumb, Bradford, she told herself, but she didn't move. For this moment, she was a part of what she'd always wanted. The Haynes family circle widened enough to admit her. The fantasy of being loved for herself had finally come true. And for tonight, she was going to live it for all she could.

## Chapter Thirteen

The women cooed like doves. Craig watched from the doorway of the nursery as Elizabeth, Rebecca, Sandy and Jill hovered over the bassinet.

"She's beautiful," Jill said, touching her finger to the infant's tiny hand.

"Just like her mother," Rebecca said.

"Better." Sandy straightened and winced. "She looks just like her dad." She shifted her weight. "I'd forgotten how much this hurt. I'm too old for this giving-birth stuff. Next time Kyle can do it."

"Next time?" Elizabeth raised her eyebrows. "You're thinking of having another one?"

Sandy smiled. "I think Kyle would like to, but I'm not so sure. This makes four kids. We're going to talk about it."

Jill glanced up and saw Craig in the doorway. "You want to come see?" she asked.

He shook his head. "You go ahead."

He'd already spent the better part of an hour hold-ing the perfect little girl. Staring down at her red, wrinkled face had given him an odd feeling. He wanted a daughter.

Of course he loved his boys and he wouldn't trade them for anything, but a girl would have been great. He frowned. Although he wouldn't want one like Krystal.

"What are you so serious about?" Jordan asked, coming across the second-story landing and pausing beside him.

Craig shrugged. "Just thinking."

Jordan glanced into the nursery. "You'd think with all the kids running around here, they'd get tired of new ones being born."

"Sorry, it doesn't work that way. Every kid is spe-cial."

Jordan looked skeptical. "You've got three already. Are you trying to tell me you want another one?"

"Maybe," he said, watching Jill.

She smiled down at the baby. He read the longing in her eyes, although he doubted anyone else saw it. "You think it's true?" he asked.

"What?" Jordan wanted to know.

"The curse. You think the real reason we had four generations of boys is none of the men loved their wives?"

"I don't know. What do you think?"

Craig pushed off the door and walked over to the railing. From here he could see Louise climbing the stairs, and beyond her to the first floor. Travis and Kyle were downstairs, playing some kind of tag game with several of the children. Shouts of laughter and snatches of conversation drifted up to the second floor.

"If the curse is true," Craig said, "it doesn't say much about my marriage to Krystal."

"You got a divorce. What did you expect? You don't divorce someone you're in love with."

"Are they still gawkin' at that child? I swear, a body would think they'd never seen a baby before." Louise reached the top of the stairs, then crossed to the nursery. She placed her hands on her hips. "You women need to let the poor thing sleep. She's not going anywhere. You can look at her later."

Craig stared after her and grinned. Louise was a force of nature. She was in her mid-forties, with short blond hair and a smile that invited the world to share her joke. Her clothing was a little eccentric, with mismatching colors that somehow managed to look right. She dressed to emphasize her impressive hourglass figure and didn't look like anyone's idea of a mother, but she'd helped out Travis and Elizabeth for nearly two years. When Austin and Rebecca had their baby, she'd gone to stay with them for several weeks. Now she was going to help Sandy and Kyle.

"Go on with you now," she said, flapping her arms.

Elizabeth, Rebecca and Jill slowly walked into the hallway and started down the stairs. Sandy lingered by the bassinet.

"How you feelin'?" Louise asked, touching Sandy's arm. "Everything hurt?"

"Just about." Sandy's smile trembled at the corners. "I'm way too old for this."

"Nonsense. You're just the right age. You've done yourself proud." Louise pulled her close and held her.

Craig turned away, suddenly embarrassed for intruding on an obviously personal moment. He glanced at his brother and saw Jordan scowling at the two women.

"What's wrong?" he asked.

Jordan shrugged and shifted so he was leaning against the railing. "Don't you find it odd that Louise is a part of the family?"

"I hadn't really thought about it. Travis hired her years ago, while he was still a bachelor."

"I know. But she's always around at family events. We don't know that much about her. We don't know who she really is."

"She's just Louise. What's the problem?" Craig frowned. Jordan didn't usually take a dislike to someone without good reason.

Jordan glanced over his shoulder. Louise looked up. Their gazes locked. An emotion that looked very much like pain crossed the older woman's face. Then Sandy spoke, drawing Louise's attention to herself.

"What's going on?" Craig asked quietly.

"Nothing. It's old news. It doesn't matter anymore. If it ever did."

"Damn it, Jordan, just tell me—"

"Hey, you two wanna play football?" Kyle called from the first floor.

"Sure." Jordan headed for the stairs.

"You're not going to tell me, are you?" Craig asked, following him.

"It doesn't matter anymore. I shouldn't have said anything."

There was a secret between Jordan and Louise. But what could those two possibly have in common? Before Craig could try to figure it out, he was hustled outside.

Travis and Kyle were acting as team captains. All the children were standing in front of them, obviously willing themselves to be picked first.

"Danny," Travis said.

Danny whooped loudly and jumped next to his team captain. "Look, Daddy, I got picked first!"

Craig smiled. "I see. Good for you."

Kyle picked Michael, Austin's adoptive son. The boy called on Rebecca, but she threw up her hands and said she wasn't going to play so he picked Austin instead.

Danny yelled, "Jill!"

She thought for a moment. "All right. I'll play."

Craig moved toward her. "The games sometimes get rough."

Travis nudged him with his elbow. "Don't worry, Craig, I'll take care of her."

"Me, too," Danny said, grinning.

He wanted to protest, but he didn't have the right. Jill gave him a "see there" look and went to stand next to Danny. She chose C.J., Austin chose Jonathan, and so it went until everyone had a team. Elizabeth and Jill were the only women playing. The kids varied in age and skill level, but none of that mattered. They were out here to have fun. It was warm in the sunny afternoon. Everyone was in shorts and T-shirts, except, of course, for Rebecca, who wore a sundress.

Travis hiked the ball to Jordan, who threw it long. Craig kept back, trying to make sure no one got hurt. Especially not Jill.

She was so tiny. She wore a bright blue T-shirt tucked into white shorts, so she was easy to spot in the shifting mass of players. She darted and ran. At one point, she nearly caught the ball. C.J. dove for her legs and knocked her down. They tumbled together like puppies, Ben and Danny joining the fun. Jill came up laughing. She ruffled Ben's hair, then tickled C.J. until he begged for mercy. Danny stood up and tugged her to her feet. Still smiling, she rejoined the game.

She touched Craig's arm as she jogged past. "What I lack in size, I make up for in speed and agility."

"I see that," he said.

Eventually he relaxed. He went out for a pass and caught it, giving his team the first score.

As he walked back for the kickoff, Jill fell into step with him. "You didn't tell me you'd made all-American in high school. I'm very impressed."

He wanted to puff out his chest with pride. "Yeah, well, it was a great time in my life, but I don't use it as an introduction."

"Did you play football in college?"

"Some. But six feet isn't all that big there."

Jordan called her over to hike the ball. She waved and darted away. Craig slowed as he watched her have a whispered conversation with his brother. Jordan bent low and placed his hand on her shoulder. She stared intently, nodding every few seconds. Craig felt his fingers bend into fists, even as he told himself Jordan would never make a move on Jill.

"You're falling hard, buddy," Austin said, reading his mind.

Craig forced himself to smile. "You fell first."

Austin looked at his wife. "Thank God. She's the best thing that ever happened to me."

Craig had spent countless weekends with his family, but this was the first time he remembered having to fight constant waves of envy. He envied Kyle and Sandy their beautiful daughter. He envied both his married brothers and Austin their happiness. He didn't begrudge them what they had, he just wanted to know how he could do it, too. And this protective jealousy Jill inspired. What did that mean? Was he starting to really care about her, or just turning into a jerk?

"Ready?" Jordan called to the team.

Jill bent over the ball. Jordan stood right behind her, his hands brushing the inside of her thighs. Craig took a step toward them.

"Thirty-two, thirty-two, hut, hut, hut!"

Instead of snapping the ball, Jill picked it up and started to run. Michael and Kyle got her first and grabbed her around the legs. One of the kids slipped and went careening into the pile, pushing everyone off-balance. They tumbled together. The tackle got bigger. Craig started toward them. Jill was on the bottom.

Jordan reached her first. He moved people aside until he finally pulled her out. She was dazed, but still smiling.

"I guess you're too little to play with the big boys," he said, lifting her up in his arms.

"It's the story of my life."

Before Craig could do something stupid like challenge Jordan to a fight, Jordan walked toward him, then Craig lifted Jill onto his shoulders. "You'd better keep her out of trouble."

Craig reached up and grabbed her thighs to hold her in place. "You okay up there?" he asked.

"I like the view. Am I too heavy?"

He chuckled. "Hardly. Did you get hurt in the tackle?"

"No, I'm fine."

Jill shifted to keep her balance. She'd never been on a man's shoulders before, but she liked it. She wasn't kidding about the view. She could see everything.

She rested a hand on Craig's head. His hair was soft and springy beneath her fingers. He held on to her thighs, and the feel of his fingers brushing against her bare legs sent tingles all through her body.

They moved to the sidelines to watch the game.

"What do you think of all this?" he asked as Danny was handed the ball and started to run.

"You have a wonderful family. I've never known brothers who are as close as you four. It's terrific."

"We got lucky about some things, although we fought like hell when we were growing up."

"I think all kids do. The question is, are you there for each other when you're needed? And that answer is yes. I know your three boys watch you and their uncles. They're learning a good lesson."

They concentrated on the game for a few minutes. She enjoyed the way Craig's boys played with the other kids. And seeing the Haynes men in action, she was starting to see the similarities and differences. C.J. was very much like his youngest uncle, Kyle. An easygoing charmer. Ben was a little bit more like a cross between his dad and Travis. And Danny... She frowned. Danny was going to be his own man.

Craig tried hard to treat the boys equally and not show favoritism, but if he were to admit any at all, she suspected Danny would be his favorite. He always took extra time with the boy. Maybe because Danny had grown up with no memory of his mother, he'd bonded more with his father.

The other team made a touchdown, tying the score. Jill tapped Craig on the shoulder. "I must be getting too heavy. Please put me down."

"You don't weigh anything," he said as he swung her to the ground. She sat under the shade of an oak tree. Craig settled next to her.

"This is great for the boys," she said, watching Ben catch a ball and run several feet before being tackled.

"Yeah." Craig leaned against the base of the tree. "It's been too long between visits. I get so caught up in work, I forget how good it feels to come back to Glenwood. The boys and I need this connection with family."

She glanced over her shoulder at him and smiled. "In a couple of weeks I'll remind you it's time to come back."

He touched her back with his hand, his fingers lingering as they slid down her spine. "You do that."

Warmth curled in her belly. The heat had very little to do with sexual desire and almost everything to do with the comfort of belonging. She'd thought she'd found something special with Aaron and his girls, but comparing that to this group of caring people was like comparing a single raisin to a gourmet banquet.

She was starving for their love and caring. Every part of her called out to join in. To be part of the circle. Funny, she'd been married to Aaron and she'd never felt as if she fit in. Maybe, in her heart, she had sensed he didn't love her. She knew that she'd never fully trusted him, although she'd spent years trying to convince herself she did.

With Craig, she didn't have to do any convincing. She trusted him implicitly because he was a kind, decent man. His incredible body and knee-weakening good looks were just a bonus to the real treasure of the man himself.

"Everyone has noticed that Ben's lost weight," Craig said. "He's real proud. I can see it in the way he walks. It's like he's a different person. He's more friendly, more outgoing. He's also more patient with the younger kids."

"I think he was always outgoing, but the weight made him self-conscious." She scooted back to lean against the tree. Craig put his arm around her and pulled her against him. She rested her head on his chest.

"I noticed C.J. isn't so much of a smartmouth these days. Danny has more confidence."

"They're growing up," she said.

"Maybe. But I think it's because of you."

Pleasure filled her. "Really?"

"Yeah." He drew in a deep breath. "You've had an effect on me, too, Jill."

The grass was soft under her bare legs. Above them, the sky was a brilliant blue. The sounds of shouts and laughter from the football game carried to them. She absorbed them all, saving them to remember later.

His arm was like a warm band of protection. She continued to rest her cheek on his chest, not only to listen to his heart, but also to avoid his gaze. She wasn't sure she wanted to have this conversation.

"We can't pretend it didn't happen," he said. "Maybe I should say— I can't. Making love with you meant something. To me, at least."

That got her attention. She tilted her head so she could look at his face. "Of course it meant something to me, too. I don't give myself lightly. You're the first man I've been with since my divorce."

"I wasn't saying that. We have to deal with what we did. There are ramifications of making love."

*Making love. Lovers.* Lovely words, but did they apply to this situation? Hadn't she and Craig both admitted to just reacting?

"A temporary romantic relationship will upset and confuse the boys," she said. "I don't want to be responsible for that. They've been through enough."

Craig stiffened and dropped his arm from her shoulders. "A temporary romantic relationship?"

"It couldn't be anything else," she blurted out.

"Why not?"

"Because..."

Because anything else was too terrifying to consider. If the sex became lovemaking, then her heart would be at risk. She would care more. She would fall for him. Once again she would be admitted because she was convenient, not because *she* was loved. This time, being used would destroy her.

"Because you don't really care about me," she said. "You're just reacting to the situation."

"You sound very sure of yourself."

"I am."

"How do you know it's not more than that?" She'd been able to read his expression for quite some time, but now his dark eyes and firm mouth gave nothing away.

She fumbled for words. "Because... That is..." She cleared her throat. "You can't expect me to believe anything else. What are you trying to say? That you've been single all these years, suddenly I show up and poof, you're healed? After hating Krystal and not trusting women, you want to make a commitment? I don't think so."

Her temper flared and she shifted until she was kneeling next to him. "It's all so convenient. That's what I resent the most. You're hinting at a relationship just about the time that everything is settling into place at home. The boys like me, you like me, so what better way to keep me where you want me than with terrific sex and the promise of something permanent in the not-to-be-named future?"

Suddenly she *could* read his expression, and he was damned angry.

"I'm not your ex-husband," he said, his voice low and cold. "If you think I am, you don't know me at all."

She twisted her fingers together. "I know, Craig. I'm sorry. You're not Aaron. You're also right about me not knowing you. We don't know each other very well. That's part of the problem. I thought I knew him and I was wrong. What if I'm wrong about you, too?"

"No," he said. "This isn't about me, it's about you. You want me to be a jerk. You want to believe I'm just like him because then you don't have to risk anything. You want me to be willing to make a commitment, but what do you have to put on the line?"

"That's not fair," she said hotly.

"Isn't it? Doesn't this truth thing go both ways?"

"I would never do anything to hurt you."

"How do I know that? My ex-wife was the most dishonest person I'd ever met, yet I'm willing to give you a chance. Why can't you do the same?"

He made it sound so reasonable. She didn't want to think she was being unfair. She'd never meant to be. "I don't know what to say."

He rose to his feet and towered over her. "I don't know what we could have had between us, but I was willing to give it a shot. I know it's hard to believe that after all this time you're the first woman who's turned me on, but it's true. And I don't just mean about sex. I mean about everything. Being with you—"

He broke off and shoved his hands in his pockets. "Hell, it doesn't matter."

She wanted to tell him that it did, but he wasn't listening to her anymore. She'd taken care of that.

"You say you don't want to confuse the children, but I think the person you're really afraid for is yourself," he said. "You're the one who's confused. Maybe you picked Aaron on purpose. Maybe you wanted someone who would use you so you wouldn't have to deal with the consequences of a real relationship."

She stood up and glared at him. "How dare you? You have no right to say that to me."

"Tell me one thing, Jill. You're a bright woman. You held a responsible job. Why couldn't you see what a jerk Aaron was? Why did you stay with him? It was easy, wasn't it? Life is always easier when you get to hold a piece of yourself back. It's giving everything away that gets so damn messy."

He turned on his heel and started for the house. She wanted to go after him, but she didn't know what she was going to say. Accuse him of being a selfish jerk? Hard words to speak when there was a very good chance that he was right . . . about everything.

## Chapter Fourteen

Jill added the eggs, oil and the prune mixture to the dry ingredients, then stirred until everything had blended together. Last she dumped in the nuts. After spooning the quick bread into the pan, she popped it in the oven and set the timer. As much as the boys complained about prune bread, they managed to devour nearly the whole loaf in one sitting every time she made it.

She glanced at the clock and saw she had a few minutes before she had to leave to pick up Danny at school. C.J. and Ben were both spending the afternoon with friends.

Jill walked through the family room, pausing to straighten a pile of magazines. The house was never in perfect order, but she didn't mind. Better for everyone to be happy than the edges of the books lined up with the front of the shelf. Craig had wanted to keep the cleaning service, so she didn't have to worry about scrubbing the bathrooms, but with five people in one house, there was plenty of other work to keep her busy. Especially now that Craig was home most evenings.

The last man who had been trying to cheat the elderly drivers had finally been arrested, and Craig was back on a regular schedule. He was home for dinner more often than not. At first it had been odd having him around, but she'd grown used to talking to him at the dinner table. They spent time with the boys, helping with homework, reading or playing games. She felt like a necessary part of a team. Which was odd because she and Craig were barely speaking to each other if they happened to be alone.

Other people made it safe. When the final arrest had been made, several of the senior citizens Craig had been trying to protect had invited him and his boys over for dinner. He'd brought Jill along. She'd loved the evening. She and Craig had sat next to each other and chatted. But as soon as they returned home and the boys went to bed, there was nothing to say.

She grabbed her purse from her bedroom and walked out into the garage. After pushing the garage door button, she waited for it to finish opening, then put the sport-utility vehicle into reverse and backed out.

The tension had started after their weekend in Glenwood three weeks ago. Neither of them wanted to talk about it. So they avoided the subject and each other. It was easier than facing the truth.

As she pulled up to the stop sign, she knew she had only herself to blame. Craig had wanted to talk about it. He'd wanted to consider the possibility that they might have a chance at a relationship, but Jill couldn't do that. She couldn't risk the pain. But even as she hid behind her fears, she wondered if Craig was right.

Had she chosen Aaron deliberately, knowing that it probably wouldn't work? Had she kept a piece of herself back from him and the girls? Had it been easier to live in the pretend world than to risk finding and possibly losing real love?

She didn't want to think that about herself. Everyone had failings, but no one liked to think about them. And to have Craig be the one pointing them out to her... She pressed on the gas and shuddered. Yet there was a part of her that knew he was right.

She *was* a smart woman. She had hidden the truth from herself. She'd gone into the marriage because it was easy and she'd stayed because it gave her an excuse not to try again.

She glanced in the rearview mirror, but instead of the car behind her, she saw only ugly truths. She gave so much to Aaron and the girls, but she gave because of what she wanted back, not because of what they needed. Oh, she cared about them. There were nights when missing the girls kept her up. But she rarely thought about Aaron.

The divorce had been painful to her pride, but losing her husband hadn't touched her heart.

She pulled into the line of cars already waiting in front of the school. The children had just been let out and most came running toward the vehicles. A few paused to chat with friends until sharp honks reminded them that someone was waiting. Jill scanned the children, looking for Danny. She finally spotted the little boy walking slowly across the grass.

She frowned. Danny usually ran, skipped or jumped when he was going somewhere. Walking was too boring. As he approached, she opened the car door, then took his books and set them in the back seat. He reached for the seat belt without saying anything.

"Danny, do you feel all right?" she asked.

"I guess."

She touched his forehead, then his cheeks. He didn't feel warm. "Are you tired? Do you think you're coming down with something?"

He shook his head.

She stared at him. He hadn't really been himself for several days. Now that she was thinking about it, she'd been noticing odd things on and off for about a week.

"Is there a problem with your Pee-Wee team?"

"No. I'm doing good. I might get to play third base." For a moment he smiled, and the Danny she knew returned. Then, just as quickly, his smile faded and he was gone.

"Your brothers are visiting friends this afternoon. It's just going to be the two of us. What would you like to do?"

He shrugged. "Nothing."

"I'll help you with your hitting if you want," she offered.

"No thanks." He stared out the side window.

Not knowing what else to say, she started the car and drove home. Once there, Danny ate half a piece of still-warm prune bread, then completed his math sheet. He didn't have any more homework, so he excused himself and went to his room.

Fifteen minutes later, Jill couldn't stand it. She climbed the stairs, went to his closed door and knocked. "Danny, may I come in?"

"Okay."

She opened the door and stepped inside. He was sitting in the center of his bed, hugging a ragged teddy bear. One of the animal's ears was missing and the fur had been rubbed off its paws. Danny looked so alone and sad. She sank down next to him and gently drew him into her arms.

"Tell me what's wrong," she said.

He didn't speak.

She rocked back and forth, holding him. He was small and slight. He continued to clutch at his bear. The sound of slow, steady breathing filled the room. She stroked his soft hair and waited.

Finally he sighed. "I'm not big enough," he said softly.

"For what?"

"For everything."

"You're big enough to get dressed on your own. Big enough to eat. Big enough to go to school, to play ball, to watch TV. You're big enough to get into trouble."

He raised his head and looked at her. He wasn't smiling. His light brown eyes were wide and filled with misery. "I'm not as big as C.J. and Ben."

"But they're older than you. You won't be as big as them until you're all grown up."

He shook his head. "I'm smaller than they were."

He slipped out of her embrace and started for the door. She followed. In the hallway, on a narrow section of wall next to the computer, were several horizontal lines with names next to them. She hadn't noticed them before. They showed the boys' heights at different ages.

"See," he said, pointing. "There's Ben when he was seven. C.J. was even taller." He leaned against the wall. He was definitely a couple of inches shorter. "I'm going to be seven next month. I won't grow enough in time to be as tall as them.''

Jill knelt on the carpet and pulled Danny close to her. ''Honey, people grow at different rates. Look at your uncles and your dad. You'll catch up. If not this year, then soon. Even if you don't, it's still all right. You don't have to be tall. You're wonderful just the way you are. Besides, didn't we decide that the best things come in small packages?''

But Danny didn't smile at her joke. He clung to her, sobbing as if his heart was broken. She held on, murmuring words of comfort, wondering why she ever thought she would be able to take this job and not get involved.

That night, after the boys were in bed, Jill asked Craig if she could speak with him. Evenings were the worst for the two of them. As soon as they were alone, the tension in the room climbed to an unbearable pitch. Usually they compensated by ignoring it. They were painfully polite in choosing television shows or movies to watch. Sometimes they just read, but that, too, was fraught with pitfalls. There was the choice of music, the volume, who used which lamp, the problem of chuckling at a funny part, then deciding whether or not to explain the humor.

Often, Jill sat staring unseeingly at the pages of her book, willing herself to find the courage to talk about what had happened between them. She kept thinking that if they could discuss the intimacy they'd shared, they would be able to find a new level of understanding. If they couldn't be lovers, they could at least be friends.

The problem was, she wanted to be lovers. She hadn't been able to think of anything else since they'd returned from Glenwood. Night after night she relived those wonderful hours with Craig. He was the kind of lover most women only dreamed about. Gentle, considerate, patient, and as much concerned about her pleasure as his own.

She kept remembering him telling her they could give the relationship a chance. Her fear got in the way of that one. So where did that leave them?

It would have been easier to forget everything if they hadn't gotten along so well in the other areas of their lives. If they'd disagreed over how to discipline the boys, or if he'd hated her cooking or was dating someone. But none of that was true, which made pretending to be immune to him even more difficult.

"I need to talk to you about Danny," she said, standing in the center of the family room. "If this is a good time?"

"Sure." He put down the book he was reading and motioned for her to take a seat on the sofa.

She sat a couple of cushions away and angled toward him. The overhead light illuminated him clearly. She could see the faint gray at his temples, the stubble darkening his cheeks. His expression was politely interested. Not by even a flicker of a lash did he give away what he was really thinking.

Now that he was on a regular schedule, he changed out of his uniform when he got home from work. She'd finally grown used to seeing him in jeans and a shirt, although the sight of worn denim caressing his thighs still had the ability to make her heart race.

Tonight she ignored the soft, faded material *and* the way it hugged his muscles. She kept her attention on her hands.

"What about Danny?" he asked, prompting her.

"He hasn't been himself for the past week or so."

"I thought I noticed something. I asked him about it a couple of days ago, but he said he was fine."

She glanced at him. "I didn't realize you'd seen it, too."

"I was going to mention it, but there wasn't anything to say. I thought maybe I was imagining things. Obviously I'm not."

"No. This afternoon he didn't want to do anything. He just went in his room, sat on his bed and hugged his bear."

Craig frowned. "I don't like the sound of that. He'd practically relegated that to the closet. So what's the problem?"

She smiled. "Actually it's nothing to worry about. He showed me the wall by the computer where you keep track of the boys' heights at different ages. He's concerned that he's shorter than both Ben and C.J. were when they turned seven. His birthday is only a few weeks away, and he knows he can't catch up. I told him that everyone grows at different rates of speed. He'll catch up eventually. I think he feels better now. He was more cheerful at dinner. But maybe you could talk to him and tell him he's perfect the way he is. Maybe..." She trailed off.

Craig wasn't paying attention to what she was saying anymore. He stared past her, eyebrows drawn together as if he were wrestling with a difficult problem. A muscle twitched in his cheek. Something dark and painful passed through his eyes.

"Damn," he said softly. "I didn't want it to come up like this."

Cold fear rippled down Jill's spine. "Like what? Craig, what's wrong? Is he sick? Oh, God, he doesn't have something wrong with him, does he?"

When he didn't speak, she leaned forward and grasped his forearm. "Answer me, damn it. What's wrong with Danny?"

Craig drew in a deep breath. "Nothing. He's not sick. At least not that I know of. He's fine." He glanced down at her hand and touched the backs of her fingers. "I swear to you, Jill. It's not that."

Slowly she released him. Worry had formed a knot in the pit of her stomach. At his reassurance, it loosened a little, but didn't go away. "Then what is it?"

"Can we please not talk about this?" he asked.

She stared at him, not sure how to answer. "If you prefer, but I'd like to help."

"No one can help.... Hell, you might as well know the truth."

He pulled free of her touch and looked straight ahead. He braced his elbows on his knees and rested his head in his hands. "I don't know how tall Danny is going to be when he grows up. I don't know what he's going to look like or what he's going to want to be. I don't know anything about him."

"I don't understand."

"Danny's not my son."

Jill stared at him, uncomprehending. Not his son? Danny? Little Danny with the big eyes and the smile that— The smile that didn't look anything like his father's.

"Wait a minute," she said, half to herself. "That's crazy. Sure he doesn't look as much like you as the other two, but he has some of Krystal's features. The shape of his eyes. If you adopted him—''

He straightened and shook his head. "We didn't adopt him. He's Krystal's. He's just not mine."

She opened her mouth, but didn't know what to say. Not his? That was crazy. "Then how did you get him?"

"I didn't plan it, that's for damn sure." He leaned back against the sofa. If his hands hadn't been curled into tight fists, she might have thought the telling didn't affect him. But the white knuckles and straining tendons gave him away. She ached for him.

"Krystal and I had been separated, but still in the same house," he said. "Not the best way to live or bring up kids. Ben was five, C.J. barely two. She didn't bring her men home. I used to tell myself that was something. God, I was a fool."

"I'm sorry," she said softly.

"Me, too." He closed his eyes. "I told you before she'd been unfaithful from the beginning."

"Yes."

"Once we'd finally started talking about getting a divorce, she went wild. Coming in at all hours of the night, usually drunk. Men started calling here. I hated it and her. Then one night, she came on to me. I was immune by then, and she was furious. She finally blurted out she was pregnant and had planned to pass the kid off as mine. But when I wouldn't cooperate, she was forced to tell me the truth."

Jill shuddered. Craig's pain filled the room. She wanted to comfort him the same way she'd comforted Danny earlier that afternoon. But Craig wasn't a six-year-old boy. She drew her knees up to her chest and wrapped her arms around her legs.

"At first I thought she was going to have an abortion," he continued, opening his eyes, but not looking at her. "She didn't. I don't know why, and I never bothered to ask. As her pregnancy started to show, she became less active, sexually, although she still went out at night."

"You never asked who the father was?"

"No. I told her I didn't care. In my heart, I was curious, and hurt, but I didn't want her to know. She asked to stay until the baby was born, then she'd move out. She'd decided to give it up for adoption. I agreed. Ben and C.J. didn't really understand what was going on. I tried to shield them from her as much as possible."

He glanced at her and grimaced. "I couldn't disconnect from her, though. When her time came, I drove her to the hospital, but instead of leaving I stayed. What a sucker I was. I hated her, but even she deserved someone there. Then they brought me this tiny baby and placed him in my arms. Krystal hadn't bothered to make any arrangements. I saw her staring at me and then I knew. She'd planned it all along. She'd known I would take in her child. I never despised her more than I did at that moment. But I couldn't blame the kid for what his mother had done."

"You did the right thing," she whispered, too stunned to do more than take in all that he was telling her. Danny wasn't his. She couldn't believe it. He'd never even given a hint. Of course, being Craig, he wouldn't ever slight the boy. He'd had her convinced Danny was his favorite.

"I couldn't let him go to strangers," he said. "Besides, by then Krystal had explained her pregnancy to the boys. They were expecting a baby brother or sister.

After she left the hospital, she got her things and that was it.''

Craig shifted uneasily on the sofa. He already regretted his confession. Jill was staring at him as if he'd just rescued an entire classroom of children from a burning building.

"I'm not a hero," he said harshly. "Don't start thinking I am."

"What would you call it then?"

"Making the best of a bad situation. I did what any decent person would have done. Keeping Danny was the right decision. I didn't trust Krystal to actually give him up. Do you know what that kid's life would have been like with only her as a parent?"

"He would never have survived."

"Exactly."

The room was silent for a moment. Jill looked at him, studying him as if they'd just met. The lamp behind her made her red hair glow, as if touched by moonlight. Her delicate features were so different from Krystal's obvious and flashy beauty. Why couldn't he have fallen for someone like her instead of Krystal? Then he remembered the boys, and he knew that whatever his ex-wife had cost him, it was worth every payment because he had them.

"Are you going to tell Danny?" she asked.

"Maybe when he's older. I know he already feels a little different. I don't want that information weighing on him, as well. Besides, as far as I'm concerned, Danny is as much mine as Ben and C.J."

"Do you know who—" She paused and shrugged. "You know."

"No, I don't know who his father is. Krystal said she didn't know, either. I don't know if she was lying, but it doesn't matter now. When Danny was born, I had him tested for drug addiction and AIDS.'' He swore. ''I had myself tested, too. Just to be safe. Hell of a thing for a husband to have to do because his wife is a slut. Everything came back negative. I know we got lucky. The way Krystal was living her life, who knows what could have happened. But that's over now.''

He was ashamed of his past and talking about it brought everything back. He just wanted to get away.

He rose to his feet. Jill stood up and moved close. ''I'm so sorry,'' she murmured.

''Don't be. It's done. We survived.''

''You did better than that.'' She stared up at him. Tears clung to her lower lashes.

''Stop,'' he said, touching his finger to the single tear that escaped. ''It's not that bad.''

''I can't believe she did that to you. And her children. To walk away from them like that. Didn't she know what a precious gift they are?''

''Appreciation was never one of Krystal's best qualities. Besides, it's over now. The boys are fine and I am, too. I'm going to make damn sure I'm never in that situation again.''

''Life doesn't come with guarantees.''

''Maybe not, but next time I'm not taking any chances.''

## Chapter Fifteen

Craig heard soft voices in the hallway, followed by muffled footsteps in the hall. He finished fastening his belt, then opened his bedroom door. Ben and Jill had already reached the front door and were heading outside for their morning walk. He followed after them and arrived at the front door just as they started stretching. He pushed aside the front-window drapes to watch.

It was a perfect late-spring morning. The sky was clear, the air still with just a hint of coolness. Dew coated the lawn, making the individual blades of grass glisten. Pansies and marigolds provided bright color along the walkway.

Ben waited impatiently by the sidewalk. He shifted his weight from foot to foot and motioned for them to get going. Jill laughed. She shook out each leg, then moved toward him.

They were both wearing shorts and T-shirts. His once-pudgy son had slimmed down. According to Jill he'd already lost fifteen of the extra twenty pounds he carried. With his new eating habits and increased activity, the rest would be gone by the end of summer.

Ben had lost more than weight. He'd changed from a sullen boy who never wanted to participate in anything to a funny, outspoken charmer. He would never match C.J.'s natural ability, but he was a close second.

As Jill and Ben walked down the sidewalk, she wrapped her arm around his neck and dropped a quick kiss on his head. The boy responded by giving her a fierce hug.

Craig felt a sharp pain in the center of his chest. Why hadn't he seen the potential danger? It should have been obvious from the beginning. Everything about Jill's personality screamed that she was someone who gave fully. She could no more hold back than she could stop breathing. He'd hired her to take care of his sons and she'd done so completely, without thought of her feelings. He wondered if she knew she'd given away her heart.

He let the drapes fall back in place. He would have expected her to be won over by C.J.'s charm, or Danny's sweetness, but it was his oldest she related to the most. Maybe it was because they were both wounded. Maybe it was because a person most appreciated that which she had worked to achieve. Whatever the reason, at the end of summer, Jill Bradford was going to find it difficult to walk away.

He should have been pleased. Thoughts of keeping Jill around occupied most of his day. She'd made a place for herself in all their hearts. If he searched the world, he doubted he would find a woman more different from Krystal. Whereas his late wife had only taken, Jill preferred to give. Krystal thought of herself, Jill thought of others. Even in bed, they were nothing alike. Krystal had orchestrated those times as if they were a staged event. She'd been interested in drama, experimentation and results. Cuddling to be close, touching for the sake of simply touching had been as foreign to her as fidelity.

Jill gave her body with the same easy selflessness as she gave her heart. She savored the heat and passion of lovemaking, yet lingered over the softer, gentler pursuits.

He wanted her. He needed her. He couldn't imagine life without her. He'd sworn next time he wasn't taking any chances, yet he wanted to take this one. Was that love?

He wanted it to be, yet it seemed too easy. He'd lived six years of hell with Krystal and six years of being alone. After all that time was he supposed to believe he would find someone just like that? Meeting Jill had been a quirk of fate. If her friend Kim hadn't eloped after agreeing to take care of the boys, he and Jill wouldn't have met. Was it possible that some cosmic force in charge of love had arranged things so poorly? If by chance she'd been gone that morning, or had refused the job, then he would have spent the rest of his life searching for what he'd already lost.

He didn't want to think about that. He crossed the living room and entered the kitchen. Jill had put on coffee. He poured himself a mug and sipped the steaming liquid.

There were no easy answers to their situation. They'd both been burned. He regretted telling her the truth about Danny. If they were to take a chance on a relationship, he didn't want it to be because she thought he was some kind of hero. He wasn't. He was just a man and father trying to do the best he could. He wasn't trying to prove anything.

He wanted her to love him for himself. He leaned against the counter and took another sip. Ironically, that's exactly what Jill wanted, too. She wanted to be loved for *her*self.

They were both afraid, both hurting, both terrified of and desperate for love. Who was going to risk it all first?

He put down the coffee. He already knew the answer to that. The hard part would be convincing Jill that his feelings were about her and not just about finding a substitute mother for his children.

"We're doing better," Jill said when she finished counting. "Only fifteen bags for this trip to the grocery store."

Groceries covered the countertop. Her biweekly shopping trips still left her stunned by the amount of food this family consumed. She knew it was going to get worse. When the boys were teenagers, they would eat nearly twice as much. She sure hoped Craig's stock in Austin's company continued to perform well. He was going to need the extra income.

Ben strolled into the kitchen and eyed the bags. "Did you buy low-fat cookies?" he asked.

"Of course."

"Thanks." He grinned.

Although the boys came with her to the market, they hung out by the hot-rod magazines or played video games. She'd quickly found it was easier if they stayed busy and away from her. If they followed her through the store, they were constantly adding things to her cart and she was constantly pulling them out.

"There were some new fat-free hot dogs, so I thought we could try those," she said.

Ben frowned. "What's in them?"

"Turkey and—" She thought for a moment. "Maybe it's better if we don't ask too many questions."

He grabbed the grocery bag on the end of the counter and put it on the kitchen table. Then he reached inside and pulled out a huge bunch of bananas. He put them in the fruit bowl.

"Jill, there's this, uh, dance at school next week. I sort of have to go. It's part of my P.E. grade."

She glanced at him. Color stained his cheeks. He focused on emptying the bag and didn't look at her. Her heart went out to him. Growing up was tough.

"I'm sure you'll have fun," she said.

"I don't know how to dance."

"I'm not the greatest, but I'd be happy to help."

He cleared his throat, then shrugged. "Okay. Thanks." He dug out a bag of apples and walked them over to the fridge. "Um, do you think—" He cleared his throat again.

"What?"

He shrugged.

She carried cans of tomato sauce to the pantry and stacked them on the shelves. Then she paused by the refrigerator and rested her hand on Ben's shoulder.

"You have done a wonderful thing these last couple of months. You've changed the way you eat and how you treat your body. You're active and that's the key to maintaining your weight. This has been a hard lesson for you, but you've learned and you're going to be fine.''

He looked at her. His dark eyes were cloudy with confusion. ''Yeah?''

''I promise. Do you know what your friends are wearing to the dance?''

''A shirt maybe. No tie, though.''

''Do you want to get something new? I'm sure your dad would agree.''

''Okay. I don't think any of my good trousers fit me anymore.'' He closed the fridge door and leaned against it. ''Will girls want to dance with me?'' he asked, his words coming out in a rush.

She wrapped her arms around him and pulled him close. She could feel his spine and shoulder blades. She glanced up.

''Darn it, anyway, Ben, stop growing. I swear you're another half inch taller.''

He smiled. ''You're just short.''

His smile reminded her so much of his father that her heart nearly stopped. She touched his cheek. ''Ben, you're going to be a heartbreaker, just like your daddy. Be kind to those little girls at the dance. Be sweet to them, tell them they're pretty and treat them with respect. If you do that, they'll follow you anywhere.''

''Yeah?''

''I swear.''

''Thanks, Jill, I—'' He broke off and hugged her tight. He was getting stronger and practically squeezed out all her air.

When he released her, she coughed a little. ''In another couple of years you'll be able to pick me up.''

''I already can.'' He approached. She ducked away.

"I don't think so," she said. "And let's not test your theory."

He grinned. A lock of dark hair tumbled across his forehead. She brushed it away, then pointed at the grocery bag still on the table. "Fold."

"Yes, ma'am."

She continued unpacking food and laundry supplies while Ben talked about his day. As she listened, her mind raced. What was Craig going to say when he found out that Ben was going to his first dance? It was a rite of passage, the first sign that his oldest was on the road to becoming a man.

Jill was glad she was going to be here to see it. She would have to remember to check the camera for film. She wanted to get plenty of pictures. In fact, she should take pictures of all of them. Children changed so quickly. Especially at Danny's age.

Danny. She paused, a bag of frozen vegetables in one hand and a half gallon of ice cream in the other. She'd barely seen Craig since he'd told her the truth about his youngest. It had been a couple of days, but the information still astounded her.

Danny wasn't his son. She didn't know which shocked her more—the fact that Krystal had intended to trick Craig into thinking it was his, that she'd been willing to give up her child for adoption or that Craig had taken the boy in and treated him like one of his own.

"Jill?" Ben held open the freezer door.

She looked at the frozen food she held. "Oh, thanks. I was just thinking."

"I guess."

She gave him a quick smile. "You can go outside with your brothers."

"I don't mind helping."

She tossed him the empty bag and reached for the next one. Cereal. These boys went through more cereal than any ten normal people could eat. She pulled out the boxes.

What astonished her the most was that she'd assumed Danny was his favorite. There was something special about Craig's relationship with his youngest. Now she knew what it was. Craig was an honorable man. He would do his best by the boy and that meant making sure he never had a hint that he was different. In time, he would need to be told, but only when he was old enough to handle the information. In the meantime he was growing up surrounded by love.

"What's in here?" Ben asked, pulling out a white plastic bag.

Jill turned toward him and bit back a gasp. How could she have forgotten? "Just girl stuff," she said, trying to sound calm.

He shuddered as if he'd touched bug guts, then tossed her the bag. It circled lazily thought the air. A square pink-and-white box slipped free and tumbled to the ground. She and Ben reached for it at the same time. She tried to cover the lettering with her fingers, but he got there first. He handed her the box.

The front door opened. "Ben, are you comin' or what?" C.J. called.

"Go ahead," Jill told him and sank into one of the kitchen chairs.

When he left without a backward glance, she told herself he hadn't seen anything. She hoped she was right.

After tossing the box on the table, she read the front panel: Accurate Home Pregnancy Test.

It was unlikely, she told herself as the familiar panic welled up inside. They'd used protection. Which sometimes fails, a little voice whispered. The odds were against her being pregnant, she silently argued. Except she was late. Very late.

She should have started her period about ten days ago. There hadn't even been a hint of anything. Which meant the stress of everything had affected her, or she was going to have a child.

A baby. She leaned back in the chair and closed her eyes. If she was, what would she do? What would Craig say? Would he think she had tried to trap him, much as Krystal had? After all, she'd been the one coming on to him.

As always, the thought of her wanton behavior made her blush. She buried her face in her hands. She hadn't planned for them to do anything. Of course, she'd thought about making love with Craig. How could she live with him day after day and *not* think about it? But thinking and doing weren't the same thing. Still, when he'd walked in on her in the bathroom, it had seemed so right.

It hadn't even been about finding love. Instead, she'd suddenly gotten tired of feeling lonely. Was that so bad? Did she deserve to be punished for one night of comfort?

Since returning from Glenwood, she and Craig had been involved in an elaborate dance of avoidance. Except for that night when he'd confessed the truth about Danny, they hadn't had a single personal conversation. She was still reeling from his accusations. In the past week, she'd tried not to think about them, but she couldn't think about anything else.

Had she deliberately chosen Aaron so she could hold some part of herself back? Did she find it easier to exist in impossible situations because she secretly wanted to be disappointed? Was she so afraid of giving and receiving genuine love?

And what about Craig? He came from a long line of failed marriages. The Haynes family didn't have a great record when it came to relationships. Yet look at what was happening now. Travis and his wife. Kyle and Sandy. Was it Craig's turn? Was it hers? How did she feel about him?

She picked up the box and stared at it for a moment. If she didn't love him, was she strong enough to walk away even if she was carrying his child?

A baby. She smiled as tears sprang to her eyes. A child of her own. It was a dream come true.

She brushed her eyes with the back of her hand. A baby wasn't her whole dream, she admitted to herself. She'd also wanted a husband. Someone she loved and respected. Someone she could trust and admire. Someone who would cherish her. Had she already found that?

If only... If only she could know his feelings. She stood up and grabbed the pregnancy kit. As she headed into her bedroom, she knew it didn't matter. Even if Craig admitted he cared about her, how was she going to trust him? How would she know that he wasn't just interested in having a mother for his children? She'd already been burned like that before.

She placed the pregnancy kit inside the medicine chest. She knew there wasn't an easy solution to the problem. There was no way Craig could prove that he wanted her and not just the convenience of having her around. She would have to take a step of faith. She wasn't sure she could.

Summer was fast approaching, then it would be September. Her condo lease would be up, her job would be waiting. Would she stay or would she go? Could she walk away from Craig and the boys? Could she risk being used once again?

How much of her confusion was fear of the past repeating itself and how much of it fear of love? Until she answered that question, she knew she wouldn't be able to decide.

"Dad?"

Craig looked up from the book he was reading. It was nearly ten. "What's wrong, Ben? Don't you feel well?"

His oldest stepped into the bedroom and shrugged. "I'm fine. I just can't sleep."

Craig patted the cushion next to him on the small sofa in front of the fireplace in his bedroom. He placed a bookmark in his book and set it on the table. "Are you worried about your dance next week?"

"A little, but I think it's gonna be okay." Ben plopped down. He pushed up the long sleeves of his pajama top and sat cross-legged in the corner. "I think I saw something, and I don't know if I should say anything or not."

"Okay. What did you see?"

Ben looked at him, then ducked his head. "It's about Jill."

Craig's stomach clenched. Was something wrong with her? Was she ill? Was she leaving? "What about Jill?"

"We were putting away groceries a couple of days ago. I was helping, and she had this plastic bag. She didn't want me to touch it. She didn't say that, but I could tell." He paused. Color stole up his face.

What had he seen? Birth control? The thought gave Craig a jolt of hope. Maybe Jill was willing to admit she had feelings for him. "Then what happened?"

"I sorta tossed it to her and this box fell out. I swear it just fell on its own. I wasn't trying to do anything wrong."

Craig leaned over and placed his hand on his son's shoulder. "I know you weren't. It's all right. What did you see?"

Ben stared at him. "I'm not sure. It said Home Pregnancy Test on the label. Is Jill gonna have a baby?"

Even as conflicting emotions raced through him, Craig forced himself not to react. He didn't want to frighten or confuse Ben and he didn't want to get either of their hopes up. He knew the boys wanted Jill to stay permanently.

"I don't know if Jill's pregnant," he said. Could she be? They'd used a condom. Of course, condoms occasionally failed. Pregnant? A baby.

"Are you going to say anything?" Ben asked. "I don't want her to think I was prying."

"She knows you wouldn't do that, son. I'll talk to her."

Ben nodded, then rose to his feet. "If she has a baby will she have to leave?"

"No. She won't. She can stay right here."

Ben nodded. Craig wasn't sure if the boy knew who the father might be. They'd talked about sex several times over the past couple of years. Ben had a clear understanding of the conception process. Craig thought about reassuring him that there wasn't a strange man in Jill's life, but then he figured he'd better talk to her first. If she was pregnant—

Ben closed the door quietly behind himself. Craig sagged back against the sofa. A baby. He grinned. Hot damn. He hadn't seriously thought about having another child, but at that moment he realized how much he wanted one with Jill. A girl, just like her mother.

A girl. He sobered quickly. Would it be a girl? Had the curse been broken by love?

He'd spent the past six years hiding, waiting for something certain. Instead, life had given him the gift of Jill Bradford. Given a choice between his precious sure thing and her, he knew what he would choose. Jill. Always Jill.

He was finally willing to take a chance. All he had to do was convince her this was about her and not the children.

He stood up and started for the door. As he reached for the handle, he froze in place and swore. If she was pregnant, she would never be able to accept his love. She would assume any declaration by him was about the baby and his feelings of responsibility. After what he'd told her about Danny, she would be even more cautious about getting involved with him.

She wanted to know it was about her and not the children or the pregnancy. Somehow he would have to find the words. Now that he'd finally figured out he'd been given a second chance, he didn't plan to blow it.

## Chapter Sixteen

Craig headed for the stairs. He wasn't sure what he was going to say to her, but he prayed he would find the words once he got there.

He crossed the dark family room. There was a light shining under her door. He knocked softly.

"Come in," she called.

He opened the door and stepped into her bedroom.

She sat on top of her bed, with the small television tuned to an old movie. When she saw him, she reached for the remote control and flipped off the set. Her eyes were wide and green, their expression questioning. She gave him a half smile.

"What can I do for you?" she asked.

Words failed him. He knew he wouldn't be able to find the right ones, anyway. How could he explain love and caring when he'd just figured it out for himself? How could he make her understand the emptiness he'd felt inside and how she'd managed to find her way in to fill every crevice of need? How could he tell her that she was the most loving, giving person he'd ever met?

He crossed to the bed and stared down at her. Without conscious thought, he reached for the hem of his T-shirt and pulled it over his head. Then he waited for her reaction.

He braced himself for her rejection or for her to calmly tell him they had to talk about this first. He even told himself she might slap him for being so presumptuous. Instead, she rose on her knees and pressed her mouth against the center of his chest.

Jill knew this was a mistake. She even knew why Craig was here. But she could no more have turned him away than she could have turned back time. They needed to talk and try to figure out what they were going to do. The logical part of her brain told her they should talk *first*. The rest of her body, on fire from the moment he'd walked into her room, slammed the door on logic and begged her just to feel.

She complied. She touched his warm skin, running her fingers across his shoulders and down his arms. She kissed his chest, his flat nipples, his belly. The waistband of his jeans rested just below his belly button. She dipped her tongue inside and teased with a quick flick of dampness.

He groaned. "Do you know what you do to me?"

"If it's anything like what you do to me, we're both in trouble," she said.

He reached for her, tugging on her arms until she rose to her feet. With her on the bed, she was taller. She grinned and wrapped her arms around his neck. "Now I've got you where I want you."

"And I've got you."

He gripped her around the waist and stepped away from the bed. She caught her breath and wrapped her legs around his hips. Instantly her damp, hot center came in contact with his arousal.

She clung to him as he spun them both around in the room. When she was too dizzy to do more than hang on, he slowed and pressed his mouth against hers.

Their lips brushed together, moving slowly in a dance of sensation so sweet, she wanted to weep. She parted and he swept inside. Fiery need cascaded through her, sensitizing every part of her body, making her tremble in his embrace. If he hadn't been supporting her, she would have slipped to the ground.

He sat on the edge of the bed. Her legs hugged his thighs. As she traced the rippling muscles in his back, he unfastened the buttons down the front of her shirt. When he'd tugged the garment free, he flipped open her bra with a quick flick of his fingers.

He cupped her curves, then sank back on the mattress, taking her with him. She landed on her hands and knees, her head slightly higher than his. He took advantage of the situation and reached up to suckle her. At the first moist touch of his mouth on her sensitized taut peaks, her arms began to tremble. She had to hold in a moan.

"Don't," he murmured against her skin. "Don't be quiet. The boys can't hear us from here."

"They can if I start screaming," she said in a gasp as his thumb and forefinger teased her other nipple.

He chuckled. His warm breath fanned her flesh. He moved his free hand between them and rubbed her damp heat. She was frozen in place, caught between two pleasures so intense, she thought she might perish.

He tilted his head slightly so he could reach her other nipple. His fingers caressed her breasts, stroking the soft undersides. Between her legs, he continued to slip back and forth, bringing her closer to her moment of release.

She rocked in rhythm with him, urging him to do more, but frustrated by the layers of clothing between them. When she couldn't stand it anymore, she straightened and reached for the button at the waistband of her jeans. Craig raised his eyebrows, then stretched out lazily, lacing his hands behind his head.

"Don't look so damn smug," she muttered as she crawled over him and pulled off the rest of her clothes.

"I can't help it. You're cute when you're turned on."

"Gee, thanks."

He released one hand and patted his belly. "Come on back."

She knelt next to him and started to lift her leg over his waist. He grabbed her hips. "Not there."

He urged her up until she was beside his shoulders. She stared down at him. "Here?"

"Yes." He reached for the pillows and pulled them out from under the bedspread. After slipping two under his head, he drew her over him, so she straddled his neck. He reached up and parted the damp curls, then touched his tongue to her most sensitive place.

Jill closed her eyes and fought back a scream of pure pleasure. She'd never done it exactly like this before. The new position made her feel exposed and vulnerable, but at the same time heightened her pleasure. She felt as if Craig could see all of her.

She braced her hands on her thighs and began to rock in counterpoint to the quick flicking of his tongue. Every fiber of her being focused on that tiny point of pleasure. She could feel herself collecting, tensing, readying for the moment of ecstasy.

He grabbed her hands and pulled them down so she could hold herself apart for him. She continued to thrust back and forth, urging him faster, deeper, harder. The passion grew. She was caught up in the intensity and barely noticed him shifting beneath her. The bed rocked as if he was moving.

Just as she came within a heartbeat of her release, he stopped. With a quick, fluid movement, he turned her on her back and kicked off his jeans. He'd already worked them halfway down his thighs. Before she could protest or even lose her passion, he plunged deeply inside her, filling her until she thought she would explode.

She opened her eyes and found him watching her. Passion filled his dark eyes, passion and something else. Something warm and wonderfully tempting. If she'd been able to think or do anything but remind herself to keep breathing, she might have called it love.

But she couldn't do anything else right now. She could only react. He braced his hands on either side of her shoulders. His powerful legs and hips thrust him inside her, then he withdrew in a rhythm designed to drive her over the edge of sanity. Within seconds, she was as close as she'd been before.

Even as the ripples of ecstasy swept through her and her body convulsed around his, she felt him achieve his release. She forced herself to continue to hold his gaze, staring in wonder at the pleasure tightening his features, at the way he exposed all of himself to her. As she wrapped her arms around his shoulders and her legs around his hips, holding him tight, she felt the first prickle of tears.

He held her while she cried. "I'm s-sorry," she said shakily. "It's j-just—"

"You don't have to explain," he said. "I understand."

She was glad someone did. It didn't make sense to her.

Gradually, his murmured words and the slow stroking of his hands against her skin comforted her. She pulled back and stared at him.

"It's never been like this before," she said.

"I know. For me, too." He shifted so he was lying next to her, then pulled her on top of him. He ran his fingers through her hair and traced the length of her spine. "I remember the first time I saw you. At Kim's."

"Hmm, me, too."

"You were naked."

She tried to sit up, but he held her against him. "I was not."

"You were naked under your robe."

"Oh." She felt her cheeks heat. "That."

"Yes, that. You made it very difficult for me to hold a rational conversation. How was I supposed to talk to you about my children when your breasts were swaying back and forth like that? Don't ever answer the door like that again."

She giggled. She'd thought the robe covered her fine. Apparently, she'd been wrong. "I haven't flashed anyone else that I know of."

"Good."

He sighed. She felt the rise and fall of his chest, then she closed her eyes and listened to the sound of his heartbeat. Images sprang to mind. Bits of conversation, time they'd spent together. A shiver raced through her.

"You cold?" he asked, reaching for the bedspread.

"No. Just an aftershock." She bent her knee and ran her foot up and down his calf. "Craig, we have to talk."

"I know."

She hadn't thought it would hurt this much, but it did. The exquisite pain filled her until she didn't want to breathe. But she had to. And she had to say the words. "Ben told you about what he saw."

"Yes."

So he knew about the pregnancy test. That was why he'd come to her. Damn. Of course that was the reason, but she'd really hoped it was something else. Something he'd thought of on his own.

"I like you, Jill," he said slowly. "I respect you."

"I feel the same way." But liking and respecting weren't loving. Her heart tightened a little. She kept her eyes closed, wanting to pull away, but knowing he wouldn't let her.

"You make me feel alive," he went on. "I'd forgotten what that felt like. I've been going through the motions for years. I've been lonely. Until I met you."

Oh, God, she wanted it to be true. She hadn't known how much until this moment. She curled her fingers into her palm and bit down on her knuckle.

He continued to stroke her hair. His other hand cupped her buttocks and squeezed gently. "I guess I don't have to tell you that you turn me on."

If her answering laugh sounded a little like a sob, he didn't seem to notice.

"I've been scared," he said. "That's not something I'm proud to admit, but it's true. You've helped me change that. I've seen that I've been hiding from the boys and that's wrong for them and for me. They need me around almost as much as I need to be around them. I was looking for a sure thing, with them and with love. But life doesn't work that way. Sometimes you have to be willing to take chances. I'm willing, Jill. I love you. I want to marry you.''

She raised her head and glanced down at him. If only he knew how much she wanted that to be true. Just hearing the words... believing them even for a second. It was a million times more wonderful than she thought it would be.

His dark eyes were bright with emotion. If only she could believe.

''I love you, too,'' she whispered. When he started to speak, she covered his mouth with her hand.

''Let me finish,'' she said, then paused. ''I—I guess I've loved you for a long time. Maybe from the first time I saw you with the boys. It would be easy to accept your proposal, but I can't.''

''Jill—''

''No. It's my turn. I can't do this again, Craig. I can't do the right thing for the wrong reason. I can't afford to be second-best.''

''You wouldn't be. This isn't about you being pregnant.''

''But if Ben hadn't told you about the test you wouldn't be here right now.''

''Maybe not at this minute, but soon.''

She slid off him and sat on the edge of the bed. ''I don't believe you.''

''I want you in my life,'' he said. ''The boys want you. It's not about the things you do. Hell, if it makes you feel better, I'll hire a housekeeper and a nanny. We just want you. I want you."

"I can't spend the rest of my life wondering if it's real."

He sat up and grabbed her shoulders, then turned her toward him. "I knew you were going to be difficult about this. How can one small woman be so damned stubborn?"

"Just lucky, I guess." But she couldn't make herself smile.

"Jill, I love you. Please believe me."

"I want to," she said. "If you only knew how much." He had no idea how much. But it wasn't to be. She needed to know they were talking about an honest affection and not simply obligation.

"I want to marry you," he insisted.

"You don't have to. I'm not pregnant."

She wanted to be a coward and look away, but she forced herself to stare at his face. She searched carefully for the flicker of relief and the verbal backpedaling as he tried to withdraw his proposal.

But Craig didn't look relieved. Instead, something amazingly like disappointment crossed his features. "Are you sure?" he asked, his mouth turning down at the corners. "Couldn't the test be wrong?"

"You sound like you *want* me to be pregnant."

"Of course I do," he said forcefully, shaking her gently. "What did you think this whole damn conversation was about? I want to marry you and be with you. I want to break the Haynes curse and have a daughter who looks just like her mother. I want it all, Jill, but only if I can have it with you."

The shaking started from the inside. She blinked several times, sure he must have misunderstood. "I'm not pregnant," she repeated.

"I got that."

"And you still want to marry me?"

"Of course. I love you."

"Even without the baby?"

"There is no getting through to you," he said with exasperation, then hauled her close and kissed her.

She hung limply in his arms as his lips pressed against hers. Thoughts raced through her mind. He knew she wasn't pregnant. He still wanted to marry her. He wanted to marry *her!*

She surged against him, knocking him off-balance. They tumbled back on the bed, a tangle of arms and legs.

"You mean it?" she asked.

He took her hand in his and stared into her eyes. "Jill Bradford, I love you more than life itself. I want to make love with you until we're both so old our bones are threatening to crack. I want to wake up next to you, I want to see you grow round with my child. Will you marry me? For better or for worse, for richer or poorer, as long as we both shall live?"

She grabbed him by the back of his head and pulled him closer. "Yes," she said, and kissed him. "Yes, yes, yes."

He laughed. "The boys are going to be thrilled. They love you very much."

"I know. I love them, too."

He touched her face, then ran his thumb across her lips. "I meant what I said about the baby, Jill. I'd love to have a child with you."

"I want that, too."

"Maybe we can get started on it right now."

She smiled. "Maybe we already did."

At his frown, she giggled. "I'm not pregnant, Craig. We didn't use any protection."

He drew his eyebrows together, then relaxed as the realization dawned. "I didn't think about it because I thought you already were pregnant. Why didn't you stop me?"

"I'm not sure. I wasn't paying attention. Maybe I wanted it to be true."

"If not this time, then next time," he promised.

"Or the time after that," she said.

He moved his hand over her breasts and grinned as her breath caught. "As many times as it takes," he agreed. "It's not as if it's hard work or anything."

He reached between her thighs and touched her quivering skin, then entered her.

She wrapped her legs around his hips and drew him closer. "I love you," she whispered. "For always."

"For always," he echoed, then led them on a journey that would seal that love forever.

\* \* \* \* \*

Dear Reader,

*Part-Time Wife* is my very first book for Silhouette Special Edition's THAT SPECIAL WOMAN! I am thrilled and honored to have the opportunity to share my story with you.

Heroines have a chance to shine as THAT SPECIAL WOMAN! My heroine, Jill Bradford, has many qualities that make her special. Jill's not perfect. Like most of us, she has assets and flaws, a couple of physical features she's not happy with, and a deep down desire to find true love. Fortunately for her, the man of her dreams happens to be Craig Haynes, the oldest of the brothers in my HOMETOWN HEARTBREAKERS series.

My thanks to those of you who have written and told me how much you're enjoying the series. The Haynes family has become an important part of my life and it's going to be difficult to let them go. Look for Jordan's book, *Holly and Mistletoe* in December 1996.

If this is your first HOMETOWN HEARTBREAKERS then you're in for a treat. These men are going to make you laugh, make you squirm and remind you of all of life's possibilities. Enjoy.

Happy reading. My best to you and yours,

Susan Mallery

# This July, watch for the delivery of...

An exciting new miniseries that appears in a different Silhouette series each month. It's about love, marriage—and Daddy's unexpected need for a baby carriage!

Daddy Knows Last unites five of your favorite authors as they weave five connected stories about baby fever in New Hope, Texas.

- **THE BABY NOTION** by Dixie Browning
  (SD#1011, 7/96)

- **BABY IN A BASKET** by Helen R. Myers
  (SR#1169, 8/96)

- **MARRIED...WITH TWINS!**
  by Jennifer Mikels
  (SSE#1054, 9/96)

- **HOW TO HOOK A HUSBAND (AND A BABY)**
  by Carolyn Zane
  (YT#29, 10/96)

- **DISCOVERED: DADDY** by Marilyn Pappano
  (IM#746, 11/96)

Daddy Knows Last arrives in July...only from

DKLT

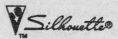

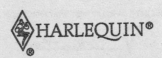